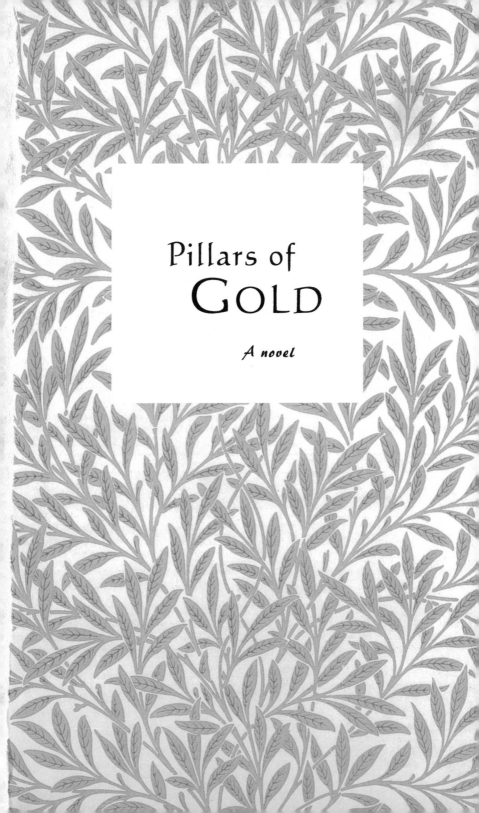

Pillars of
GOLD

A novel

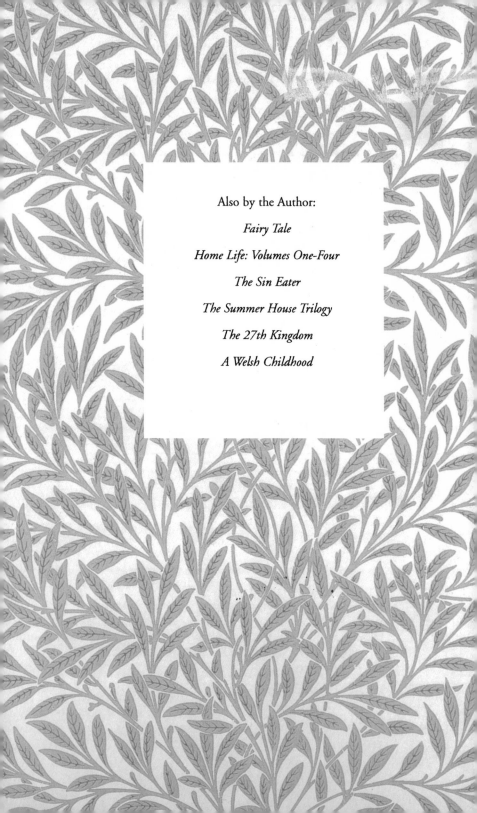

Pillars of
GOLD

A novel

Alice Thomas Ellis

Moyer Bell

A Common Reader Edition

Wakefield, Rhode Island & London

Published by The Akadine Press / Moyer Bell

First Edition

**LIBRARY OF CONGRESS
CATALOGING IN PUBLICATION DATA**

Ellis, Alice Thomas
  Pillars of Gold / by Alice Thomas Ellis.
  —first ed.

  p.   cm.
  1. Female friendship—England—London—
Fiction. 2. Missing persons—England—
London—Fiction. 3 Women—England—
London—Fiction. 4. London (England)—
Fiction. I. Title.
  PR6055.L4856 P55   2000
  823'.914—dc21   99-054174
  ISBN 1-55921-284-5 CIP

Printed in the United States of America.
Distributed to the trade by Publishers Group West,
1700 Fourth Street, Berkeley CA 94710
800-788-3123 (in California 510-528-1444).

To
Janet, Alan, Jean, Alfred, Sarah, Isobel, Tom,
Tom L., Tural, several Sams and Chris

The fields from Islington to Marybone,
To Primrose Hill and Saint John's Wood,
Were builded over with pillars of gold;
And there Jerusalem's pillars stood.

Pancras and Kentish Town repose
Among her golden pillars high,
Among her golden arches which
Shine upon the starry sky.

William Blake

Schoolchildren fled in terror, weeping as police dragged the blood-stained body of a woman from the canal at Princes Lock last Tuesday afternoon at 2 p.m. A teacher when interviewed stated: 'It was disgusting, the police showed no sensitivity at all . . .'

Brian, having read this paragraph in last week's local newspaper, put it aside, rose to his feet, kissed his wife with the words 'Love you' and left – ostensibly for his place of work.

His stepdaughter also left – ostensibly for school. She had not sat down to breakfast, preferring to eat a handful of dry Puffkins while she sought her shoes, nor did she utter any words of affectionate farewell, not being one for dissimulation. She was at that age.

She walked through the streets until she came to the litter of a part of town which teetered unbecomingly between abject decline and frenzied development. Here she picked her way to the bar currently favoured by herself and her friends. It was Spanish in intention and remarkably expensive, selling those spicy morsels which are given away with drinks in more liberal countries.

As it was not yet open, she sat on the step beside a broken box of rotting plums and watched the market traders going about their business: they all seemed to be in their usual mood of precarious good humour which could splinter at any moment into invective and menacing gesture. Camille took all this for granted, as she accepted without surprise the rows of adjacent stalls and shops selling leather jackets and boots, videos and sandwiches, samosas and scorched sausages. Most local commercial outlets dealt in things to wear or watch or eat. There was also a large new bookshop and several shops selling stationery and filing cabinets and offering the opportunity of faxing or photocopying documents of such significance that they must be duplicated, but Camille's mother could not buy a mop bucket or a length of elastic or a wheel of cheese without going to the centre of town. Camille, of course, did not care a bit since she had never felt the need of such things.

'Hi,' said her best friend, Sam, sitting down beside her and placing her bag of school books on an extended stain of dried urine.

'*Good* morning,' said Camille jovially.

'What's wrong with you?' inquired Sam. 'You sound happy.'

Camille was disconcerted. She and her friends seldom discussed the concept of happiness: when they were not either bored or depressed they were having a good time and enjoying themselves. To Camille the word 'happy' had an archaic ring. 'Only babies are happy,' she said.

'They are, aren't they?' said Sam, beginning to giggle. 'All fat and bubbly and chubbly and cootchy-wootchy-coo.'

They clutched each other and swayed back and forth, breathless with laughter.

'Morning, girls,' said one of the younger market men, pushing an empty trolley near to their feet.

Sam said, 'Morning,' but Camille glanced at him haughtily and looked away: she considered that she had no time for the working classes, although her mother's best friend had been brought up here in the olden days before the supermarkets and the middle class had come to compete for space. She was different. Constance was Constance.

'What shall we do?' asked Sam.

'You going to school?' asked Camille.

'I got to later,' said Sam, 'or she'll ring my mum.' Sam was going to a tutorial college, where the staff tended to keep a close eye on their pupils, being moderately well paid to do so, while Camille was still at a local comprehensive where the teachers no longer cared much about anything.

'Bitch,' said Camille, commiseratingly.

'Yeah, well,' said Sam, who was a year older, 'but they do teach you properly.' She wore the expression of a catechumen, raw and as yet uninitiated, who dimly sees the advantages of the otherwise disagreeable course before her. Camille leaned across and dropped a rotten plum on her school books.

'You *cow*,' cried Sam, without malice: only a few months ago she would have pressed the plum into her friend's hair, but now she threw it on to the pavement where it lay easily among the cabbage stalks and traces of vomit.

'What'll I do?' asked Camille.

'You can hang round the Lock,' said Sam. 'Or,' she added, as one who makes a surprisingly original suggestion, 'you could go to school.'

'I got Social Studies,' said Camille, unanswerably.

'Yeah, well,' said Sam again. They watched a woman, who could not have been long in this country, testing a mango for ripeness: she felt it all over with her thumb, not looking at it, concentrated, unsmiling, until the stall holder, ever-vigilant, caught sight of her. The expected outburst over, Sam said, 'We should have warned her.'

'She wouldn't've understood,' said Camille. 'Grandma says this is the only country in the world where they won't let you feel the fruit.'

'Still,' said Sam, 'they let the dossers pick up the ones they throw out.'

'Decent of them,' said Camille, and again they bent over, limp with mirth. The doors of the bar opened behind them and they went in to order hot chocolate from the rather older part-time student who had learned the advisability of doing something to earn a little money and had taken several jobs as a waitress. Sam and Camille thought her hopelessly wet.

Scarlet, left alone in the house, looked at the breakfast table in horrified disgust: this feeling had first started some time before – she couldn't remember when – as boredom. She had managed to cope with it by listening to the radio, playing tapes, even turning on breakfast television until its unremitting triviality had threatened to drive her even madder than she had felt herself going already. Now she thought that if she had to clear the table once more, put the few plates in the dish-washer, put the cereal packet away, brush the crumbs from the table top, she would scream and go on screaming: scream until the plaster started to crack from the walls and the neighbours gathered to stand whispering outside the window and the cat fled in terror. She ought to feed the cat – and then there was the washing. The builder should be summoned to scrutinize the small growth on the pantry's outer wall, and her husband had informed her that the bank had made another balls-up and requested her to deal with it. Tonight they were going to the theatre.

Examining her responses to this normal catalogue of everyday events, of life, she found that she wished she was dead, had been dead for some time, so that she was used to it: and then she thought that if she had been dead for long enough, she would probably be bored with that by now. She decided that what she felt was panic, the terror of

4

being trapped not in too small but in too large a space, where too much could happen and go beyond control. She knew, from reading and from subjection to the media, that she was not alone in her distress: the world was full of nutty housewives, many of them probably just round the corner, since she lived in a district famed countrywide for feminism and madness. Some were suffering from post-parturition melancholy, some from the effects of withdrawal from Valium; many were single mothers and many the victims of spouse or 'partner' abuse.

Scarlet hated the word 'partner'. She began to make a mental list of words she hated. 'Meal' and 'choice' and 'portion' and 'mutual' and 'caring' and 'unwaged' and 'second home' and 'home'. Then she began on a list of words she liked, but all she could think of was 'fireplace'. After a while she thought of 'angel' and wrote it down on the telephone pad.

'Mum's *dumb*,' explained Camille to her friend Tim, as they sat sipping Coke on the banks of the canal. 'She doesn't understand anything.'

'You mean,' observed Tim sagaciously, 'she doesn't know you're bunking off school.'

'She wouldn't care,' said Camille.

'I bet she would if she knew,' said Tim. 'I bet she'd go bananas.'

'Well, she won't know if nobody tells her,' said Camille, but, in truth, she knew she could depend on the discretion of her friends. They would lie like flatfish to protect each other from parental awareness, and so certain were they of the rightness of their cause – which was, in many cases, the pursuit of uninterrupted idleness and pleasure – that no one could disbelieve them. They were a generation of large, well-nourished, beautiful children with silken hair, smooth skin and clear eyes. Some of them had taken drugs, but on the whole this was regarded as both old-fashioned and working-class, so swiftly do perceptions and attitudes change. On the other hand, when they got the chance, they drank more than was good for them, and they all smoked, either surreptitiously or openly, depending on where they were and the various fashions in tolerance among their parents, some of whom still smoked cannabis to the scorn of their offspring. They were all also, in one way or another, prejudiced and snobbish, although they would have denied this with their dying breath. Colour and caste were immaterial to them, but poverty they despised: not the real poverty of the dispossessed, the homeless and derelict, with whom, bizarrely, they tended to identify, but the poverty of those who were forced to work in uncongenial jobs. The maternal words 'If you don't study hard, you'll end up on the check-out counter at Tesco's' had had, if not the intended effect, the result of causing Camille and her friends to look down on shop assistants, bank clerks and bus drivers: for more recondite reasons of their own they also held in contempt estate and travel agents and people who worked in advertising. Camille's stepfather worked in advertising.

'He's such a *jerk*,' she remarked, remembering him as he left the breakfast table clad in the dark, light-weight suit which hung uneasily between an older idea of what was appropriate to the businessman and the current notion that, since it was no longer altogether cool to be a businessman, the person in the fast lane to wealth should appear relaxed and unconstrained. Brian could not bring himself to discard collar and tie but looked, always, slightly ashamed of them.

'He's nice to me,' said Tim.

'He's nice to everyone,' said Camille, '*he* thinks. He goes, "Oh, have a drink, old boy," and he thinks people like him.'

'*I* like him,' said Tim.

'You don't know him,' said Camille.

'He doesn't beat you up or rape you, does he?' asked Tim.

It had not previously occurred to Camille that he might. 'No,' she conceded, 'but he's always *there*.'

With some reluctance, for this generation was not free of sexual solidarity, Tim had to agree that he knew what she meant. His own father's mistress had a habit of always *being there*. She could be a nuisance: she would remind his father that his exams or a dental appointment were due, or comment adversely on the state of his room. Not, thought Tim, because she greatly cared for his welfare but because she liked interfering. He was rather sorry for his father.

'They mean well,' he said.

'Oh, Tim, you're so *Christian*,' said Camille.

'You should meet my friend Chris,' said Tim. 'You'd like him. You'd get on well together.'

'I hate men,' said Camille.

'Charming,' said Tim.

'Not you,' said Camille. 'You don't count as men.'

Just before midday Camille drifted into an even more expensive bar-restaurant further down the road. She only had about fifty pence left from the money she had borrowed from her stepfather the day before, but she hoped that the young Italian barman, who fancied her, had not yet been sacked or moved on and would give her a margarita, free. Other customers, strangers, sometimes offered to buy her

7

drinks, but it was against her principles to accept them. A small, fat, rich man sat ogling girls' legs: he was there most days and represented everything Camille most despised: she thought that he imagined he was living in a Continental fashion.

Her stepfather, who had been there since he left home, drinking coffee and mineral water and reading the papers, turned his chair slightly, so that she would not be able to see his face, supposing that one adult male back would look much like another to those of Camille's generation: his wife, he thought, would have recognized him from any angle. Thinking of this, he wondered why he was feeling guilty, since from the professional point of view he was working – that is, he was having a working breakfast with some colleagues. They hadn't arrived yet, because they had been held up in the traffic, but they would be along in time for an early lunch. This was all quite accepted, but he couldn't rid himself of the memory of his wife gazing blankly at the breakfast table with only the prospect of clearing it. Although he knew she would be bored if she was here, he still felt uneasy. His first wife had left him to become a theatrical agent because she didn't want to be just a housewife. So she said. The truth was she hadn't wanted to be a housewife at all: she had wanted someone else to do the washing and the shopping and the cooking and to mind the child while she breakfasted with clients. This had been doubly hurtful, for it meant that she not only did not want to work for and look after him but preferred his lifestyle to her own, and by implication (for she was a lazy woman) that meant that she considered what he did not to be work at all, merely a pleasurable means of making a great deal of money. He had been in the habit, as he left in the mornings, of saying, 'Well, I'm off to work now,' until one day, shortly before she deserted, she had, at those words, slammed shut the door of the dishwasher with a crash that shattered a wine glass and shouted at him: she had inquired, without much originality, what he thought *she* did all day, whether he imagined that cooking and shopping and washing and minding the child was not work, whether he supposed that she would now retire to her bed and lie there sucking chocolate bars and examining her fingernails until he chose to return for dinner. She had said much more, and while he had not listened closely, he had got the gist. He was certain that Scarlet would never behave so irrationally but could not quite rid himself of the image of the breakfast table.

There was a current copy of the local rag lying on the chair beside him: he had read *The Times* and the *Independent* and now turned to the more microcosmic news. As he was not an insensitive or a brave man, the larger items in the national dailies frequently upset him and clouded his mind with vague anxieties. He remembered the local papers of his youth, with their accounts of flower shows, weddings and the meetings of societies.

The local rag still contained these, but they were outnumbered by descriptions of neighbourhood robberies, muggings, drug-trafficking, rapes and murders. On the front page was a story about an old man who had lain dead in his council flat for eighteen months until Gas Board workers had discovered him, a blurred photograph of some local women who were going somewhere in a body to protest about something and a larger picture of a council dignitary opening some sort of centre and looking pleased with himself. The impression that things had got worse was inescapable.

There was a letter relevant to the murder item he had

seen that morning, and he read it through, frowning. The headmistress and the governors of the school named were justly irate, for, they stated with concerted vehemence, no child had witnessed the recovery of the body of a murder victim from the canal: those children who had not been making stegosauruses out of old egg boxes had been learning an Ashanti war dance, and not one had been in the playground, which was the only vantage point from which body recovery would be observable. Nor, added the headmistress and governors roundly, before appending their names, had any teacher expressed dissatisfaction with the behaviour of the police, for no teacher had been interviewed by a reporter. Brian was shocked: this was not the usual journalistic inaccuracy but downright lying. The blurring of the precise borders between fact and fantasy was one thing, untruth another.

He had to think like this because of the nature of his employment, whereby he was often required to make inflated claims for the nature and properties of the products which his clients wished to bring to the daily notice of the populace. He had learned never to say deprecatingly, as some of his colleagues thought it polished to do, that he was ashamed of his profession because that would sound as though he was, and in a way he was. He never admitted this to himself in so many words, which was probably why he had occasional attacks of breathlessness and a tendency to develop a rash behind his ears. That, at any rate, would have been the diagnosis of Scarlet's therapist.

Turning back to the local rag he learned that the police had as yet no clue to the identity of the woman whose body had been fished out of the canal. It was a terrible world where people could die and nobody would claim the remains. It happened all the time round here. He sometimes toyed with the idea of going to live in an EC country, where the streets were cleaner and the wages even higher, but he wouldn't be able to speak the language.

Camille, returning from the Ladies, observed her stepfather sipping mineral water and reading the paper and made a detour round the tables to avoid him. She could always claim this was a break period, but on the whole it was easier if her movements remained unobserved. Her Italian friend had gone from behind the bar, but his replacement was proving equally obliging. She was very soon a little the worse for drink, her pale hair untidy and her features less perfectly exquisite than they should have been. She laughed a lot.

Scarlet sat cross-legged, in the position referred to as the 'lotus', on the quarry-tiled floor of her kitchen and breathed deeply. The French windows were open upon the garden, and after a while she saw her best friend Constance vaulting the low fence which separated them and approaching her.

'You ought to try acupressure,' said Constance. 'It relieves all the tension.'

Scarlet had just thrown away a bunch of dried Provençal flowers which had adorned her sideboard for over a year and was already feeling slightly better: she thought that if only she could rearrange all the furniture, she might be cured, but it seemed too drastic a step to take.

'I suppose yoga's out of date,' she said.

'Yes, a bit,' said Constance. 'Not under the banyan tree so much, but round here, yes, it's a bit dated.'

'When did you get back?' asked Scarlet. 'I've been missing you.'

'Just now,' said Constance. 'I haven't even unpacked. Memet says when you're travelling all you need to take these days is precautions, so I've only got the one bag. Matter of fact, I'm puzzled.'

'Oh?' said Scarlet. It was unlike Constance to worry. Whenever she felt unwell or oppressed she embarked on a new course of treatment at the alternative medicine centre or ingested a new range of vitamins.

'Yes, well, you know I said you needn't feed the cat and water the plants because Barbs said she'd do it?'

'Yes,' said Scarlet, coldly.

'Well, my plants are all dead and the cat's starving, and when I went across to her place it was all locked up and there are piles of junk mail on the mat.'

'Eliot can't be starving,' protested Scarlet. 'I've been feeding him. He kept stealing Nigel's food, so I gave him a bowl of his own every day.'

'Well, the plants are all dead as a doornail,' said Constance, 'and she's not been in. It's all exactly the same as I left it.'

'She must've gone away,' said Scarlet, gratified to hear of the dead plants and Barbs's dereliction of duty, for she had been rather hurt not to be asked to mind Eliot.

'It's not like her,' said Constance, and Scarlet had to admit that she was right.

Barbs prided herself on her deep and politically informed compassion. She concerned herself about everyone – the neighbours, the tramps, the gipsies, the feral cats and the condition of the local trees. When the council had organized a festival to alert the people to the plight of Nicaragua, she alone of all the neighbours had climbed into the mobile coffee shop, which the council had provided, to drink Nicaraguan coffee and read the Nicaraguan posters which adorned the bulkheads and bulwarks of the van. She went on gay-rights marches – although, as far as anyone knew, she was heterosexual – and was wont to punch the air with her fist at moments which seemed to call for affirmation or triumph. Sometimes she also uttered a cry which she had picked up somewhere: a kind of 'Yah!' Barbs would surely never voluntarily leave a cat or a Busy Lizzie to starve.

'You seen her going in and out?' asked Constance.

'No,' said Scarlet, 'but then I don't notice much.' She found it easier to live in a faint fog, at one remove from what most people called reality.

'She's let me down,' said Constance. 'She's supposed to be Miss Kind and Caring, and she's let me down.'

'Perhaps something's happened to her,' said Scarlet. 'Did you look through the windows?'

'I looked through the letterbox and all the downstairs windows, and there's not a whisker,' said Constance. 'Nothing. No sign of her.'

'I suppose it's all right, though,' said Scarlet. 'I mean, what could have happened to her? Something must have come up, and she must have gone off in a hurry. One of her friends or something.'

'It's odd,' said Constance. 'Who'd want to have Barbs around if they didn't have to?'

'A man?' suggested Scarlet. 'Do you want decaff or camomile?'

'She may've been murdered,' said Constance. 'Or abducted,' she added as an afterthought. 'Only you'd have to feel sorry for anyone who kidnapped Barbs. She'd sit round trying to raise his consciousness. He'd have to be a stranger.'

'She wouldn't go away with a stranger,' said Scarlet.

'Yes, she would,' said Constance, 'She might feel discriminatory if she didn't.'

'There are terrible things in the papers,' said Scarlet,

vaguely. She was acting on the advice of her therapist in speaking thus. Her therapist held that it was natural and healthy for human beings to assume that bad things happened only to other people in remote areas. Scarlet did not believe this for a moment, which was why she held reality at arm's length and had to see a therapist about it. She felt she should reassure Constance, with a sane and cheerful smile, that such things didn't go on in their street, but Constance reminded her that they did.

'There's terrible things *here*,' she said. The police had only recently organized a stake-out in a house just down the road, watching and waiting for a serial murderer to call in at his mother's council flat to collect his laundry. There were regular burglaries in houses and flats, both private and council-owned. No one was safe, particularly not old ladies and single women.

'And those tinkers,' said Constance, venomously. 'They've been bringing their dogs to do their business in my front garden, and if I go to the council, d'you know what they'll say? They'll say I'm harassing the travellers.'

Scarlet regarded her wistfully. Constance had thick, coarse black hair and wore an orange scarf somehow knitted into it. She had dark-brown, shiny eyes and a tanned, muscular frame on which she hung brightly coloured blouses and skirts. She very often went barefoot in order to keep her feet in good condition, and she wore long, dangly ear-rings. She had Irish blood and gipsy blood, and one of her brothers trained greyhounds. She was thus entitled to be as forthright as she wished about the travellers, who kept camping in the council yard and various public spaces and were cordially loathed by the local residents, whether they admitted it or not. Scarlet both hated and feared them but was restrained by her class and upbringing from saying so.

14

'And the kids,' continued Constance, 'little bastards. Two of them came round a while ago and they said, "Our pigeon's on your roof, miss, can we go up your house and get it down through your loft?" I *told* them,' she concluded with a smile of pleasure at the recollection.

'Poor little scraps,' said Scarlet, regretting her words as she spoke. She feared the gipsy children because they had still, wicked faces and the swiftness of weasels. 'They've not had much chance,' she added by way of apology for herself.

'You sound like Barbs,' observed Constance. 'I'll have a camomile.'

'But what *about* Barbs?' asked Scarlet, who was finding this mystery diverting. 'Honey? Don't you think you should go to the police?'

Fifteen years ago, when Brian and Scarlet had just bought the house next door to Constance, she had regarded the police as her worst enemy, but things had changed. Now she saved her animus largely for the council, which seemed unfair, since it had permitted her to buy for almost nothing the house which her mother had rented and given her a grant for improvements. She still dealt in stolen goods when she got the chance, but the police were less interested in stolen goods than they had been in the more law-abiding times of some years before. Now, what with drugs and violence, they had their work cut out without worrying unduly about the van-loads of cardboard boxes which regularly changed hands in the market. 'Maybe,' said Constance, non-committally.

'What would you say to them?' asked Scarlet.

Constance was patient with her. 'I'd say she's not there and she should be, and we don't know where she is. I'd tell them about the plants. I'd say, I'm sure there's no real cause for worry, but I'm a bit concerned. I'd just *tell* them.'

'Do you want to telephone from here?' invited Scarlet.

'No point in telephoning,' said Constance. 'They've got a central exchange somewhere up north and they put you on hold till the local mob come in for their tea.'

Scarlet admitted that if this was not precisely the case, there was yet room for considering it probable: she had often found difficulty in summoning the aid of the force, being directed by a controller to different stations which in turn would advise her to try elsewhere. 'They've got a lot on their plate,' she said.

'I could go there,' said Constance, sucking honey from her spoon.

'Do you want me to come with you?' asked Scarlet.

'No, it's all right,' said Constance. 'I'll go round Sainsbury's on the way back.'

When she had gone Scarlet began to peel courgettes, worrying the while whether she was not doing so prematurely: if she left them thus denuded, exposed to the air, they would discolour, while if she immersed them in water, their vitamin C content would dissipate. She could cook them now and reheat them, but that, she believed, would be deleterious to their nutritional value: it would perhaps be best to entrap them, with their vitamins and trace minerals, in a china bowl enveloped in clingfilm in the coolness of the fridge, taking care that the film did not touch them lest some cancer-inducing chemical should migrate from the one to the other.

Next she considered the potatoes: in the past she had always cooked them in their skins, but recently it had been suggested that potato skins, if not carcinogenic, were yet harmful to the system, perforating the bowel or preventing it from absorbing the vital vitamins. She scraped them

16

carefully and put them in a steel pan, covering them with the bottled still water in which they would be boiled, thereby retaining the vitamin C which would otherwise have been poured down the sink.

Scarlet had thrown away all her old aluminium pans since she had learned that they might cause Alzheimer's disease, and she never used tap water for cooking for the same reason. She never drank the water from the tap and all the vegetables in her kitchen were organically grown. The chicken, which she next drew from the fridge, had, so the label proclaimed, ranged freely over a district of France before being hygienically and humanely slaughtered and packed. It somehow gave the impression that the fowl had led such a delightful and pleasurable existence that it was a positive act of virtue to eat it.

Years ago Constance's mother had kept chickens at the bottom of the garden, and when they went off the lay one of her sons-in-law had strangled them and she had given them away to the neighbours, being unable to eat a bird she had know'personally. Several of them she had given to Scarlet, stipulating that she must pluck and draw them herself. This Scarlet had done, and now she wondered how she could have: maybe you became more squeamish the further away you grew from the experience of childbirth. When her mother died Constance had turned slightly vegetarian and announced that she would never have any children since her mum had had ten and put her off the whole idea, and she gave away the chickens.

At this Brian had resigned himself to living in the district. Previously he had made Scarlet's life hell by waking every morning at cock-crow and threatening to go next door and complain: he never would have done so, since he was frightened of Constance's mum and, indeed, of

Constance and the rest of her family. He took it out on Scarlet in the same way as he avenged himself on her for the pressures at work and the demands of his first wife. Brian had given Scarlet the impression that, if it had not been for his first wife and her child, and his second wife and her child, he would have been living a life of carefree splendour in a house adjacent to the park. Scarlet had accepted that it was all her fault and endeavoured to do her poor best to compensate him for his unjust circumstances. In one matter only had she determined to have her own way: she was going to be on good terms with the neighbours for the sake of her sanity. Brian had not merely hated the cockerel but feared it since it had got through the fence and bitten him on the leg. Constance and her mum had laughed, so that he not merely feared but hated them. More than that: he had himself sprung from the upper working class and naturally despised as unclean the lower working class: his life was made a misery by their proximity, and he longed for them to be evicted or murder each other in one of their not infrequent rows.

Constance had assumed that, since she and Scarlet lived next door to each other, they would constantly be in and out of each other's houses and behaved accordingly, which had suited Scarlet very well. At that time she had known few people in the district, for they were among the first of the incomers, and Camille had been only a baby with the consequent ailments, accidents and dissatisfactions. As she could not afford to keep a nanny or an *au pair*, having permanently available a woman who had borne and reared ten children, together with a woman who had been one of them, had been to Scarlet a godsend. She sometimes thought it had saved her life as it had undoubtedly saved Camille's. When Camille had choked on an Aztec cuff-link, a sizeable piece of jewellery such as had then been fashionable, Constance's mum had held her upside down by the ankles and banged her until she disgorged it, while Scarlet had knelt in the unutterable anguish of one about to be bereaved, determining to destroy herself without hesitation should Camille not survive the experience. Constance had supervised Camille's introduction to the children of the neighbourhood, to her own nephews and nieces and those of approved families – some in which the parents were still encouraging their infants to assist on their shoplifting expeditions had been dropped from her acquaintance, as she regarded petty larceny as common and ill-advised – and had taken her to many places deemed of interest to children which Scarlet would have found uncongenial.

Scarlet had striven so to arrange matters that Brian would not be subjected too often to Constance's distasteful presence, nor Constance to Brian's lowering glances and muttered observations, the atmosphere he could create simply by being there, like one of those slow-burning mosquito repellents which make life insupportable for all the creatures of God. Although she was unaware of it, Scarlet had acted bravely, if pointlessly, in her dealings with these two, for it was she, not Constance, who endured Brian's discontent, drawing his disapproval upon herself and suffering vicariously for Constance, who cared nothing for Brian's opinion, mood or reactions. Sometimes Scarlet had a brief insight into her own attitudes to other people and would realize that she had suffered far more pain on their behalf than was necessary and that no one would ever thank her for it: this made her feel useless and extremely tired. Over the years it had become apparent that Constance considered Brian a person of little consequence and that, this being the case, she would not have minded if he had hired the Albert

Hall to denounce her as a barbarian and certainly cared nothing for his kitchen sulks and drawing-room sarcasm.

When the three of them had been together in the kitchen, the infant Camille crawling round with jam on her face and fingers, he had sat in a state of sullenness bordering on rage or had conspicuously moved about preparing food for himself, knowing quite well that his dinner was cooking in the oven. Scarlet had lost weight, sweating with the embarrassment and misery of it all, yet would not give up Constance; and when they threw parties Constance came too. After a few initial displays of outraged incomprehension, Brian had been forced to accept this as a fact of life, explaining to his colleagues and superiors, with a wry smile, that Constance was a friend of his wife's: his wife had a taste for the eccentric, since she was the daughter of a famous artist, and, oddly enough, believe it or not, Constance was a skilled silversmith. She had indeed once worked for a silversmith but had discovered that it was much easier to buy beads and acquire old pieces of jewellery, rearrange them artistically and sell them on market stalls throughout the country.

Scarlet felt relieved now that Constance was back: she had the sensation of one abandoned in a pit who sees a face peering down, aglow with friendly interest. She couldn't get out of the pit, but somebody knew she was there: her therapist gave her something of the same feeling but was far from being as much fun. Scarlet didn't care what they said about psychiatry – she got the impression that her therapist disapproved of her, simply because she needed therapy, and it was no use anyone saying anything to the contrary. Sometimes she eased the weight that lay on Scarlet's heart for an hour or two, but the relief never lasted.

Constance was Scarlet's lifeline to a world where not

everything was necessarily disastrous, a warmer world of colour and joy and even of hope. Constance, her family and friends showed forth their feelings artlessly, with simple language and gestures, seldom seeming aware of any call for emotional discretion or more than the most basic politenesses of society. Scarlet, with the sentimentality of the deprived and the perceptions of the health-conscious, admired enormously their wholesome lack of refinement, their coarse fibre, their willingness to say what they meant without deceit or searching for means of extended expression. Their world contrasted remarkably with the world which Brian perceived and had contrived to project into her own experience, a cold and bitter world of aspiration, envy and the eternal prospect of imminent financial collapse. She felt intensely sorry for poor Brian, living as he did with anxiety and insecurity, and had never seen the necessity of channelling any of her pity back into her own parched reserves. Constance said she was too hard on herself, but Constance didn't understand what Brian had to put up with, what he had sacrificed for her. Perversely, Scarlet found this one of Connie's greatest attractions.

She would soon be back from the police station and the supermarket with tales to tell, tales of Oriental complexity and splendour, of law and commerce and life on the seething streets. Constance had known the stall holders in the market all her life. She knew their names and the afflictions they suffered from, she knew the names of their children, and she was never, ever, fobbed off with inferior or bruised apples and pears or dying spinach. It was yet another of the advantages of belonging to the working class, like always knowing someone who would send her son round to unblock the sink, lay a carpet, get the cat down from the tree, lend you a van for the evening or sell you trainers and tracksuits cheap.

Scarlet could not now imagine how she had passed the week with the house next door empty and soulless: she tidied the kitchen in readiness for her friend's return and sat down to read the local paper, two copies of which had just been delivered through the letterbox. The people who took it round tended to assume that in a house of four storeys there must be two families: some of them would leave four copies.

The letter from the headmistress and governors of the primary school shocked Scarlet. She was shocked at the journalistic licence it exposed and appalled by the crime to which it referred. This was the first she had heard of it, for while Constance was away she had not felt able to accommodate the horrors revealed in the local rag and had read only the advertisements and the page called 'Eating Out'.

She was not unduly concerned about the murdered woman but was reminded that Camille spent much of her spare time slouching along the canal banks, sometimes in company, sometimes, she greatly feared, alone. If anything happens to Camille, she thought, I will kill myself. Then she remembered that her therapist had said something about that, had said that it was not for Camille that Scarlet grieved in expectation but for herself and her own pain, implying by her tone that it was really most foolish. Scarlet had been willing to admit the truth of her words but had ceased too soon to concentrate, her mind already elsewhere as she wondered whether, if she could express herself differently and more coherently, her therapist might not have another, and a clearer, image of her.

Her image of herself tended to change according to which mirror she had last looked into or which person she had last spoken to. The bathroom mirror was candid, almost disapproving, whereas her bedroom mirror took and returned a more indulgent view, softening lines and contours. Her mother and her husband usually made her feel plain and failed, while Constance gave her a feeling that she was, at least, adequate. Sometimes, when Constance was at her most trusting and confidential, she unwittingly endowed Scarlet with a measure of her own sense of worth and superiority. This sense was not merely one of self-confidence, since it arose in conjunction with a serene contempt for most of her neighbours and was not subjective, Scarlet reflected, and the glass reciprocated.

It was plain to her that her therapist was meticulous, thoughtful and highly trained – it was undeniable – but Scarlet increasingly found all that beside the point because her malaise had not significantly decreased with treatment, and worrying about the cost of it kept her awake at night. She had not yet learned how greatly Brian exaggerated his financial problems in order to keep her in line. His apprehension arose not out of a fear that she would ruin him by extravagant expenditure but from a neurotic anxiety that if she knew how much money he had put away, she might feel free to leave him. So when they held dinner-parties Scarlet skimped on the smoked salmon, and Brian rebuked her for her graceless parsimony. Her therapist had suggested that she should speak more fully and openly to her husband, but an ancient, instinctive residue of wisdom had told Scarlet that this would be inadvisable: she had not gone through any process of transference, did not therefore regard her therapist as omnipotent, and so her suspicion that she was wasting money on her treatment was not unfounded.

Constance was, at present, the most important person in her life, for it was to her that she read out items of interest in the newspaper, with her that she shared her doubts and prejudices and to her that she described her dreams. Ideally, she knew, Brian should have been the recipient of all this intellectual and spiritual outpouring, but he was not interested, and her therapist, who should have been the other option, merely picked all the meat off her perceptions and left her with a meaningless pile of bones. Constance, by contrast, had always had someone to talk to: brothers and sisters and a mother. Even her father, Scarlet had gathered, had sometimes talked to his children, offering words of advice on a Saturday evening. She had had aunts and uncles and cousins and a parish priest, while Scarlet had had none of these.

It was all very well for Connie to say, as she sometimes did, that Scarlet's therapist might know all there was to know about psychoanalysis but clearly knew sod-all about human nature. She was someone to talk to. Scarlet, when aware that she was consciously asking her friend for advice and support, felt guilty, for she had come to believe that advice and support were commodities for which you paid professionals, rather as you paid prostitutes for love and bought your vegetables instead of growing them yourself. Everything had become a matter of commerce, negotiation and the studied application of scientific theory. Scarlet, while inwardly deploring this state of affairs, could yet see no way round it. Connie, who read widely, it wildly, held that it was all due to the Enlightenment, but Scarlet had no idea what she meant.

Camille walked down a sleazy stretch of road, where half the shops were closing as the developers quadrupled the rents, and bought herself an ice-cream to take away the taste of margaritas: it was already midday, so she had only an hour or two before she could go home, claiming that her games lesson had been cancelled because someone had felled the netball posts. When she had taken the trouble to go to school, lessons had often been called off because someone had vandalized some necessary piece of equipment. Few of Camille's schoolmates, even had they been able to read and write, would go on to a career in the sciences, since the chemistry lab had been the first to succumb, years back, when the rules had just been relaxed and attitudes to education liberalized. For a while the authorities had replaced the Bunsen burners, test-tubes, textbooks and phials of chemicals which fell victim to the ravages of the undisciplined, but they had been forced to accept defeat.

She hoped her stepfather would be home late: although she had spent most of her life with him, she regretted that her mother had felt unable to exist as a single parent, and Camille still wished that he would prove unfaithful or die. Many of her friends had stepparents, and few of them were happy about it: in their rambling and interminable discussions they would deplore the stupidity and selfishness of their elders in introducing into their homes strangers who were not of their blood and who insisted on peculiar foodstuffs and liked or disliked various types of music – whichever was most inconvenient and painful to the children of the house. Some of them even had to endure the presence of stepbrothers and -sisters, which to Camille would have been insupportable. They had certain tricks and devices by which they avenged themselves on the interlopers, but these took up time and energy and, since they were young and inexperienced, frequently rebounded on themselves, although Sam, by dint of great perseverance and the manifestation of genuine hatred, had recently succeeded in ridding her home of her mother's latest lover.

'Just think of the fairy-stories,' Sam had said. 'It never

worked, did it?' And they would see themselves as the Babes in the Wood, or Cinderella, or young princes more lovely than the morning, turned adrift on the world to seek their fortunes, while vulgar and ugly cuckoos slept in their beds and drank the top of the milk.

Camille was quite aware that her mother coped with these unspoken tensions by leaving them like that: unmentioned, if not unnoticed. She treated all the awkwardnesses inherent in social intercourse in the same way, by disregarding them. When people apologized to her for breaking a glass or making a remark which, upon sober reflection, they found themselves regretting she would smile the vague smile of the hostess who is at once too preoccupied and too superior to notice the *faux pas* of those around her.

It drove Camille mad: she would lose her temper as she had lost it when still in her pram and would wave her limbs and bellow while furious tears fell to collect under her chin. She resented being compelled to behave like this, always being the one to draw attention to the fact that all was not well, that there were idiots and enemies under their roof, eating their salt and sullying the air with their breath. She would have preferred to be a good girl who could move among adults in silence, relying on the common sense of her parent to observe and extinguish any threats to her comfort or susceptibilities. The knowledge that her mother loved her was not sufficient to quench her rage, for she felt that she had been made to grow up too soon and had no idea that her mother regretted her own inability to speak openly and lose her temper.

Her family and acquaintance would have been greatly astonished to learn that Camille considered herself prematurely grown-up, and she herself was waiting for the day when she could tame her anger into cold bitterness and frame it into phrases as cutting as tempered steel. The day she could behave like a real bitch, thought Camille, would be the day she was truly adult, and she envisaged in anticipation the bodies of advertising executives and the makers of video films lying staring with sightless eyes at the city's polluted skies, slain by the detailed revelations of her insight into their characters. Sometimes she worried that her idealism might diminish with age and that she would end up as mindless as the foe, but when she thought of her stepfather she was consoled. It was improbable in the highest degree that, with his example before her, she would ever resemble him or adopt any of his opinions. He believed, and she had once heard him say, that eventually she would, naturally, come round to his way of thinking, and she had vowed to work harder at the study of English literature in order to learn enough words to refute him once and for all. Her family, though not her friends, would have been even more astonished to learn that Camille considered herself an idealist.

'What did the police say?' asked Scarlet.

'I didn't go in,' said Constance. 'I saw DI Damplips floating about, so I went straight past. We don't want to get mixed up with him.'

'Why not?' asked Scarlet.

'Because he's bent,' explained Constance. 'He's on the square.'

Scarlet accepted this without question, as she accepted all Constance's character analyses: some dogs, she believed, had the same capacity for swift and accurate judgement. It was all to do with instinct, unsullied intelligence and an innate ability to discount the higher promptings of reason.

'He's got a string of racehorses down south,' said

Constance, 'and he didn't come by them as he was proceeding in a northerly direction on the evening of the twelfth in the course of his duty, I can tell you.'

'Hasn't anyone asked where he got them from?' inquired Scarlet, who still imagined, in her innocence, that in a developed society blatant wrongdoing could not go unobserved and unmentioned.

'Oh, Scarlet,' said Constance, sighing and sitting down.

Scarlet felt foolish and rather jealous: she knew that if she so much as failed to pay a parking ticket, the full force of the law would be upon her like a ton of bricks. 'Can't somebody do something?' she asked.

'They're all too busy fomenting riot,' said Constance. 'Do you want a herbal tranquillizer?'

'No, thanks,' said Scarlet. 'Who?' she asked timorously. 'Who are fomenting riot?'

'Them,' said Constance. They often had this sort of conversation, and Constance always made allowances for Scarlet's naivety: such slowness on the uptake was the result of a sheltered background and not necessarily a sign of limited intelligence, though she sometimes wondered. 'The government,' Constance said, 'and their mercenaries, the police. They let all the big companies go round digging holes in the road, and when people fall in and complain they say it's all for their own good, and after a while they hope the people will revolt so they can give the police guns and thin out the population, and then they'll have a police state – which is what they've always wanted – and the rich will be able to live in peace.'

'Constance!' protested Scarlet.

'It's true,' said Constance. 'There's more people in prison here than they've got in Turkey, and when there's no more room they'll put them in concentration camps and call them rehabilitation centres. Don't forget what they did to Billy.' (Although Billy had undoubtedly been guilty as charged, the evidence against him had been largely manufactured, and none of his family had ever recovered from the injustice of this.)

Scarlet felt that there was some flaw in her friend's argument but was unable precisely to pinpoint it. There was, undeniably, a spirit of unrest abroad in the air, violence and lawlessness, and corruption in the City, law courts and local councils, while the streets were foul with detritus and thronging with derelict humanity. She had, only the other day, seen a policeman and -woman exerting more force than had seemed strictly necessary on a man in the street: at the time she had assumed that he had offered fierce resistance until she had turned the corner, at which moment he had been subdued. She had race memories of Our Boys in Blue and was loath to believe them brutal. 'They're not all bad,' she said.

Constance agreed. 'Of course they're not. They're the same as Billy, mostly, but they're being manipulated from the top. I blame the Americans.' Scarlet looked at her. 'Example,' Constance elucidated. 'Telly. Our masters want a swift return to the feudal system, but they can't think how to go about it, so they're copying American methods of law enforcement because it's modern, and if it's modern, it can't be bad. Only old-fashioned's bad, see?'

Scarlet was glad that Brian wasn't present. Constance's political views nearly deranged him with fury. 'I suppose you could be right,' she said.

'Everything took a wrong turn . . .,' said Constance, who seemed inclined to continue her dissertation.

Scarlet interrupted her. 'So where did you go if you weren't at the police station? You were *ages*.'

29

'I went to church,' said Constance, 'to light a candle for my intentions.' She didn't explain what these intentions were, and Scarlet didn't ask. 'They don't believe in sin any more, did you know?'

'No,' said Scarlet.

'It's all part of the same plot,' said Constance. 'The teachers don't teach, the priests don't bother, and they're releasing all the lunatics into the community so they don't get looked after and they'll either pass out from exposure or starvation or kill people because they're mad, and then they'll be slung into prison to add to the overcrowding, and all in all it doesn't make a lot of sense. Though, I suppose, in the end it does thin out the population.'

'I suppose,' said Scarlet, doubtfully.

'I was going to have a coffee at the Greek cake shop,' Constance went on, 'but just as I was going in one of those middle-class, middle-aged ladies with a smile on her face was coming out, and whenever I see one of them I think she's going to try and sell me a poppy or something or tell me Jesus loves me. She put me off.'

'Barbs thinks women should be priests,' said Scarlet. 'I don't know why. She's not a Christian.' Barbs adhered loosely to some Eastern-inspired sect whose professed aim was universal love.

'She's an animal-righter too,' said Constance, 'and she's not a dog. Well, she *is* . . .,' she amended, 'but you know what I mean.'

Barbs was one of those not unusual women who consider themselves beautiful in the teeth of the evidence. It was probably her most annoying characteristic that in a room full of beauties she would comport herself as one with a right to be there, and there was nothing in the world that anyone could do to disabuse her. She frequently wore no make-up, and when she did she put it on wrong. Despite this she would persist in offering her face for respectful attention, interposing it between people deep in conversation and turning it up appealingly to the person serving rice-and-bean salad or pouring *sangría*.

'You can never trust a blonde,' said Constance 'not even artificial ones like Barbs. They think they look all sweet, and underneath they're as cruel as cruel. There's a nurse in the hospital . . .'

Scarlet interrupted again. 'But what about Barbs?' she demanded. 'What are you going to do? What if a mad person's murdered her?'

'Nothing,' said Constance. 'I decided to do nothing. She'll be all right somewhere.' She looked a little discomposed as she spoke, as though guilty about this *laissez-faire* attitude, but she went on, 'If her family are worried, *they*'ll do something.'

'She's got no family,' said Scarlet. 'The only ones she's got are in America.'

'Well, then,' said Constance, 'no one's going to miss her, are they?'

'You never really meant to go to the police at all, did you?' said Scarlet.

'No, not really,' said Constance, and Scarlet felt herself concurring in an age-old belief that, when it came to the point, the closing of ranks took precedence over the well-being of the stranger within the gates.

At that moment Camille came home. 'Darling,' she cried, embracing Constance. Scarlet put the kettle on.

'You've grown,' said Constance.

'Have you seen my *bust*?' said Camille, thrusting out her chest and twirling round. 'I got a new bra.'

'Very nice,' said Constance. 'Very handy for catching crumbs.'

'Where've you been?' asked Camille, still hopping about. 'You're all *tanned*.'

'Cyprus,' said Constance. 'I told you I was going. You never listen to me these days.'

'Wiv Memet?' asked Camille. Memet was the love of Constance's life, or so she claimed.

'It started off that way,' said Constance, 'but he came back half-way through. Had a job, he said.'

'Oh, poor Con,' said Camille. 'Did you miss him?'

'Not really,' said Constance. 'No, not a lot. I was staying with his aunt and her kids and her kids' kids. There's thousands of them. I had to sleep in the same room as loads of them on account of we said I was his secretary.'

'Why on earth did he come home early?' asked Scarlet.

'Why did you say you were his secretary?' asked Camille.

'They're very proper out there,' said Constance. 'His aunt would've died of shock if she'd thought there was anything going on. We even took a typewriter. I didn't use it much, though. I had a notepad and I wrote poems on it when he was talking, so they thought I was taking letters. At least, I suppose that's what they thought.'

'You don't look like a secretary,' said Camille.

'He told them things were different in England,' explained Constance. 'They swallowed quite a bit out of politeness, but they're not stupid, so I had to behave myself. It was easier when he went, in a way.'

'But why did he?' asked Scarlet again. 'Why did he come home early?'

'He *said* he had a business deal to tie up,' said Constance, 'but I think the strain was getting him down. He can't stand kids.'

'Ugh,' said Camille. 'I hate children too. They must be worse in a hot place. How could you bear it?'

'I'm used to it,' said Constance, and Scarlet thought her daughter tactless for speaking ill of children when Constance's family was so rich in them.

'I'm starving,' said Camille, wrenching open the fridge. 'There's nothing in here to eat.'

'Don't be silly,' said her mother. 'There's tons to eat. The fridge is bulging.'

'It's all *healthy* stuff,' said Camille. 'I want baked beans on toast and meringues.'

'Baked beans are good for you,' Constance advised.

'Oh, are they?' said Camille. 'Never mind. Mum, make me some baked beans on toast.'

'If you're sure that's what you want,' said Scarlet, reaching for the tin-opener. 'You musn't spoil your dinner. I'm about to put the chicken in, so you can have some before we go. I'll fry you a few courgettes to go with it, and I'll boil the potatoes now, so all you have to do is remember to put everything in the fridge once it's cool enough . . .'

A few months previously she would have gone on to implore Camille not to let her friends eat everything in the fridge. At one time Camille and her peers had moved around like soldier ants devouring all in their path. Scarlet had watched amazed as teams of youthful strangers had made unerringly for the fruit bowl, demolishing pears, grapes and even the mango which was really there for ornamental purposes, without uttering one squeak which could be construed as a request for permission. Scarlet had never thought of herself as well-brought-up, but these children of barristers, journalists, bankers left her bewildered. She hadn't complained too fiercely because that was not her nature, and also something told her that Camille undoubtedly ate other people's parents' mangoes with the same insouciance. They were no more secretive or abashed than the soldier ants would have been, gnashing their way through anything that was organic, their collective mind unclouded by doubt, guilt or the smallest hint of compunction. Open-mouthed, Scarlet had followed their progress through bread bin, fridge and pantry and, all too frequently, had had to fly to the shops to replenish her stores before Brian could become aware of the ravages. More than once they had thoughtlessly consumed the ingredients of his dinner . . .

'You dining out?' asked Constance.

'No. I'll make a chicken salad when we get back – it doesn't take a minute . . .'

'Why not?' insisted Constance.

'Why not what?' Scarlet asked wearily, 'If you mean why aren't we dining out, it's because it's a ridiculous waste of money . . .'

'You could've gone to Memet's uncle's place,' said Constance. 'Nice and central, and the food's not bad if you don't think too closely about it.'

'I don't like eating a lot late at night,' said Scarlet. 'I wouldn't appreciate it.' And she'd be sitting on the edge of her chair with a smile stitched to her face as she willed the rest of the party to get a move-on so she could go and make sure Camille was home and safe. 'Now, mind you eat these courgettes,' she said to her daughter, as she sliced them into the pan. 'They're good for you.'

'And you should eat salad every day,' said Constance. 'Every day everyone should eat at least one broad-leafed vegetable.'

Camille couldn't see what the dimensions of the leaf had to do with anything and asked whether mustard and cress were therefore worthless and was there any value in endive, all frayed and ragged as it was.

34

'Don't be silly . . .,' her mother began, but Constance silenced her with a thoughtful gesture.

'No,' she said, 'she's got something. My acupuncturist told me about the broad-leafed veg, and I didn't think to ask him what he was on about. He meant lettuce and spinach and cabbage and stuff, but when you come to think of it, there's watercress and all those titchy little herbs, rosemary and things. Maybe he was telling me lies. Maybe he's got a brother, a farmer, with a load of old cabbages to flog.' Constance had been raised in an atmosphere of intense family solidarity.

'Anyway,' said Scarlet, remembering, 'broad-leafed veg retain radioactive . . . becquerels, or something, for a long time, so even if they're good for you, they're bad for you.'

'It's the case with most things, isn't it?' said Constance. 'Nuts are full of goodness, but they make you fat, and there was a bloke once died of drinking too much carrot juice.'

'You can take it to extremes,' said Scarlet, 'this healthy-eating business.' She scraped a little butter substitute on to her daughter's toast.

Camille watched. 'Hey, I want butter. Buckets of it. That's the whole point of baked beans.'

'Cholesterol,' Scarlet warned, but again Constance raised her hand.

'No,' she said. 'There's something in butter that we need for our sex drive. Hormones or something. You shouldn't cut it out completely. I read it somewhere.'

'I don't care about my hormones,' said Camille. 'I just like butter. Don't let those beans boil. If they're too hot, they melt the butter and you can't taste it. Why do you keep waving your arms round, Connie?'

'Was I?' said Constance. 'Must be a habit I picked up abroad.'

'You reminded me a bit of Barbs,' said Camille, starting on her beans.

An image of Barbs rose unbidden in Scarlet's mind: wide-eyed and frank with the spurious and shallow candour that belonged so particularly to those citizens of the USA who had undergone analysis. They had rooted themselves everywhere with their missionary zeal – in social work, the churches, schools, groups of all kinds – preaching equality and openness and endlessly *talking*.

'God,' said Constance, hastily sitting on her hands.

At least, Scarlet thought, Camille didn't notice I've given her wholemeal bread.

'I'd better get round and feed Eliot,' said Constance. 'I got him a bit of coley, and it cost me what salmon would've cost a few years back. I keep thinking it's too good for the cat, but I can't fancy it myself.'

'It makes wonderful fish pie,' said Scarlet, 'with garlic and parsley.'

'Yes, I know,' said Constance, 'but Mum always fed it to the cat. As far as I'm concerned, you might as well eat Whiskas.'

'There's another cat gone mad,' said Camille, 'from eating cat food made from mad cows. Tim's dad's girlfriend told him. She doesn't care about the cat, she just thinks Tim's dad spends too much money on it. She says in Belgium they'd give it scraps that people didn't want.'

'Belgian, is she?' inquired Constance. 'Now *they* eat too much. I've seen them abroad, all eating too much. It puts a strain on the heart.'

'She's always fussing about her food,' said Camille. 'She thinks if people miss a meal, they'll die too soon, but she won't eat potatoes and dumplings and Belgian things. Tim sat up all night once picking the raisins out of the muesli to spoil her breakfast. He *hates* her.'

'How's Tim getting on at Westminster?' asked Scarlet, who distrusted talk of hating stepparents.

'OK,' said Camille. 'I said I'd go round and see him later when he's done his homework. Help him relax. They make him *work*.'

'How awful,' said Scarlet.

'I think they make them work too hard,' said Camille. 'It's not fair.'

'Make sure he walks home with you,' said Scarlet, 'or get a cab. I don't want you walking the streets alone. A woman was murdered only the other day, down by the canal.'

'Oh, *Mum*,' said Camille, cool with the confidence of the adolescent who knows that the rules of mortality, the risks inherent in living and going about the world, do not apply to her. 'Nobody's going to murder *me*.' She was right, as it happens, but Scarlet, not being clairvoyant, couldn't be expected to know that and resigned herself to yet another evening which would not be wholly enjoyable even had she not been going to the theatre.

'I'm going to make Memet shepherd's pie,' said Constance, 'with courgettes and cauliflower and sweetcorn.' She would, herself, have dispensed with the shepherd's pie, but Memet was a man and a Turk to boot. 'He likes English food after all that goat.'

'Goat stinks,' said Camille, for it was not so long since she had been frequently taken by Connie to children's zoos where these creatures – mostly nannies and kids – were considered suitably sized and disposed to mingle briefly with the children of men.

'It's not so bad,' said Constance, suddenly stricken with a shaft of loyalty to the culinary customs of her loved one's fatherland. 'His aunt cooks it with honey and garlic, and it's not so bad.'

'Give *me* a McDonald's,' said Camille.

'You're not to eat beef,' said her mother.

'Oh, *Mum*,' said Camille.

'Do I look all right?' asked Scarlet. She was wearing what she considered to be an ageless garment – a hip-length coat of black watered taffeta; the shoulders were rather too narrow and too sharply defined to be precisely fashionable, but the material was of most superior quality. Underneath this she wore black cotton trousers – ideally these should have been made of silk, but she felt sure no one would notice.

'You look wonderful,' said Camille without raising her eyes from the television set. She had eaten her supper and was beginning to feel hungry again.

'No, really,' said Scarlet.

Camille fell to her knees from the sofa and gave her mother's leg a patronizing pat. 'You've got a sweet little face,' she said. Scarlet, though not reassured by her words, was touched by her gesture until she saw that Camille was merely reaching for the crisp packet and had patted her in passing.

'Do these shoes go with these trousers?' she asked.

'Yes,' said Camille, her fingers deep in the crisp bag.

'You didn't look,' said Scarlet. 'Are they too old-fashioned?'

'No,' said Camille. Scarlet gave up. Only a few years before, Camille had been acutely concerned about her mother's appearance, sometimes refusing to be seen with her in public, but now it seemed that she no longer minded: she had expropriated from Scarlet's wardrobe those few articles that she felt would suit herself and had thereafter left her mother to her own devices. It gave Scarlet the impression that she had grown very old and from now on might just as well go round in her shroud.

'You look *lovely*,' said Camille, who was clad in her invariable faded and ripped blue jeans. She had many upper garments of different materials and styles which she changed according not to the weather but to her mood: she had large woollen jumpers and little skimpy vests, lacy or patterned blouses and voluminous T-shirts; shirts of chiffon and shirts of linen. She seldom wore the pretty dresses or smart suits that Scarlet bought her, preferring her rags. Most of the time she *did* look lovely, despite her apparel. Scarlet supposed she should be grateful that her daughter had not shaved her head, tattooed her nose or chosen to go around in floor-length black, hung about with chains and crucifixes like so many of the girls on the streets.

'What are you doing?' inquired Brian from the doorway. 'We're going to be late.'

'Is the cab here?' asked Scarlet, but he didn't bother to answer: her sarcasms, her rebellions, went always unnoticed, possibly because she intended that they should. 'Now, Camille, mind you make Tim bring you home or get a cab . . .'

'I haven't got any money for a cab,' said Camille automatically, and just as automatically Scarlet slipped her a fiver while Brian's back was turned. 'Thanks, Mum,' said Camille. The money would make a useful contribution should she and her friends decide to spend the evening in the pub. 'Have a nice time,' she called as the front door opened.

'We haven't gone yet,' Scarlet called back. 'I'm looking for the taxi.'

Camille pressed the clock button on the TV control. 'You'll be late,' she said.

'Where is that cab?' demanded Brian.

'I expect it's stuck in the traffic,' Scarlet apologized. 'It isn't here yet.'

'I can see that,' said Brian. Scarlet began to feel hotter than the weather merited: she was embarrassed when her husband was offensive to cab drivers, and it was now almost inevitable that he would be. She was relieved when the mini-cab drew up and the driver was not the usual small foreigner but a stern-looking English woman: Brian was not rude to people like that.

'Now, remember,' Scarlet called to her daughter, 'don't be late.'

Camille was feeling tired; the idea of going out had ceased to appeal to her, yet the prospect of staying in by herself was too sad to be contemplated: she ate another bag of crisps while she thought about it, and after a while she fell asleep. When she woke up two hours later she was aggrieved to discover that she had spent the evening alone and went to her room to listen to music.

Next door Constance also heard the music and hummed a tune as she served Memet his supper.

'You happy?' he inquired.

'It depends,' she said: she was feeling happier since Memet had arrived but would not have dreamed of telling him so. Scarlet was not altogether correct in her estimation of her friend's open nature. Even the noblest savage can give way to deviousness, should the occasion arise.

'On what does it depend?' asked Memet with a smug expression.

'On whether this poxy oven's browned the shepherd's pie or not,' said Constance. 'It's all very well for you. You can serve anything. I take a pride in my work.' Memet himself was not actually in the restaurant business, but his family was. He did not deny her assertion but smiled contentedly as Constance drew her dish from the oven. 'You,' said Constance, 'you'd be happy anywhere.'

'So would you,' said Memet, 'if I was there.'

'You don't know me at all,' said Constance. 'You think you do, but you don't. You're a very conceited man.'

'I'm entitled to be conceited,' claimed Memet, who had been spoiled by his mother.

'I'd like to know what you were up to while I was away,' said Constance. For a moment she looked accusingly at his abundant hair, his olive skin, his blameless eyes. 'Drinking, gambling and womanizing,' she surmised.

'You know me better than that,' said Memet.

Constance didn't bother to reply but sat down beside the cat, which in some ways reminded her of her loved one. After a while she said, 'I've got things on my mind.'

'Money?' asked Memet.

'I don't worry about money,' said Constance. '*You* should know me better than that. My brothers wouldn't let me worry about money – they'd always see me all right.'

'Like mine,' said Memet, competitively. 'We are both the children of peasants . . .'

'And thieves,' interposed Constance absently.

'And thieves,' Memet agreed. 'People who hang on to their land and property even if it kills them, so we've never had to worry about money and that's why we're such nice people.'

'But your dad was rich by the time you came along,' said Constance, 'and mine was dead. I had a very hard childhood, and my mum died of overwork. There was ten of us, remember.'

'My father was one of fifteen,' said Memet.

'Yes, well, don't let's play numbers,' said Constance. 'There was only four of you.'

'That's what happens,' said Memet. 'The richer we grow, the fewer children we have. We don't need them.'

'Then I must be very rich,' said Constance, 'because I'm not going to have any.'

Memet did not contradict her, for, fond as he was of her, he had no intention of marrying her. His mother wouldn't let him. Constance knew this perfectly well. Nor would her own mother have permitted her to marry Memet.

'Anyway,' said Memet, 'your mum was eighty when she died.'

'That's not old these days,' said Constance. 'She was worn out.'

'That what's worrying you?' asked Memet.

'What?'

'You said you were worried. You just said so. Just a minute ago. You said you had something on your mind, and I interrupted you.'

'Ah,' said Constance, pushing Eliot aside and brushing her lap. She considered for a moment and decided to lie. 'I'm worried about Scarlet,' she said. 'I sometimes think she's going nuts. I think she's going to have a nervous breakdown.'

'What can you do about it?' asked Memet. 'Why should you be worrying?'

'She's my friend,' said Constance, who was no longer really lying. Now she came to think of it, she *was* a bit worried about Scarlet. 'She's like a trapped animal, and she upsets me. You want to pick her up and run with her and put her safe in the loft with the apples. Every time I look at her she makes me feel guilty for not doing something about her.'

42

'What loft?' asked Memet.

'Don't act soft,' said Constance. 'You know as well as I do, in English literature the only safe place is in the loft with the apples.'

'I didn't know that,' said Memet.

'And all the money your dad spent sending you to public school,' said Constance. 'Anyway,' she added, diverted for a moment, 'where's safe for you if you don't know any English literature?'

'I don't know,' said Memet. 'My father talks about the olive trees on the hillside when he gets bored with Edmonton.'

'There you are then,' said Constance. 'Same thing.'

'We're guessing,' said Memet. 'We're second-generation. We only know what our parents tell us.'

'You mean they were probably lying or coming over romantic about the past, and, what's more, all those old poets were probably doing the same thing. You mean it was probably all shit. Not that you'd know.' Constance's countenance began to darken.

'Not *all*,' said Memet, 'but we wouldn't go back to the olive trees – not for ever, not unless we could take our money with us.'

'Makes sense,' said Constance, morosely. 'You've gone and depressed me now. You've reminded me what man is doing to the planet.'

'Really?' said Memet.

'There's not going to be room for olives soon,' Constance told him. 'Your lot are slinging up tower-block hotels all round the coast and stamping out the olive groves. I read an article about it. Makes you sick.'

'That's Turkey,' said Memet.

'Same thing,' repeated Constance.

Memet didn't argue. 'Let's go to bed,' he suggested.

'With Camo making that racket next door?' she said. 'You must be joking.'

'Make her turn it down,' said Memet.

'And Golden Delicious,' said Constance. 'The Frogs are dumping all their rotten Golden Delicious on us, and we're not going to put *them* in our loft, are we? And burning our lambs. *Alive.* They're burning lorry-loads of our lambs alive.'

'The French have a barbaric strain,' said Memet. 'Come to bed.'

'We're no better,' Constance persisted. 'If you knew what the oil companies are putting in the sea. And the atmosphere. The air here's worse than in Los Angeles.'

Temporarily Memet gave up. 'I'll make the coffee,' he said.

'Don't want Turkish,' muttered Constance. She was annoyed with herself for not stating openly what was really worrying her. Put at its simplest, it was jealous suspicion, for when she had looked through Barbs's windows she had seen Memet's straw hat sitting on the sill: he always put his hat on the window-sill. 'Where's your hat?' she asked.

Memet looked round. 'There,' he said, pointing at the window-sill.

'I don't mean that one,' said Constance, since that one was rather a foolish-looking trilby. 'I mean the straw one.'

'I dunno,' said Memet. 'I probably left it somewhere.'

'Yes, but *where?*' demanded Constance in a rhetorical whisper.

'What?' said Memet, bringing the coffee to a third flourishing boil.

'Nothing,' said Constance, 'nothing at all,' and she turned on Beethoven's Fifth to drown the noise of Camille's record player.

She wondered, as she washed the dishes and Memet lay on the sofa with his feet on the cushions, whether some ancient warlock had ever discovered a truth drug while digging around among his herbs in the dark of the moon or even whether there was not some artificial chemical compound which would produce the same result and cause her lover to come clean about his dealings with women. The truth, she mused, as others had done before her, was an elusive element, and – short of shooting them in the knee-caps, or intermittently holding their heads under water – there was little one could do to persuade people to reveal it. It was not, at present, the eternal verities which were occupying her mind but the simple gnawing question of what Memet had been up to behind her back.

'How's Mick getting on?' he asked, as she dried the dishes. 'It's about time I went to the dogs again. Give him a call and ask him for some winners.'

'Yes,' said Constance, vaguely. Mick disapproved of Memet as strongly as did the rest of her family, but Memet either didn't know or didn't care. 'He's had a run of bad luck,' she said. 'I've not seen him for some time.'

'You've got me now anyway,' said Memet. 'I'd never see you short of money. You know that.'

'Do I?' said Constance.

Memet looked at her, uncomprehendingly. Being a man, he could not understand why she should sound so doubtful. 'I'd never let you go short of anything,' he said, 'and if anybody hurt you, you know what I'd do.'

'Yes, yes,' said Constance. 'I know what you'd do. Blood everywhere.'

Memet was wounded by this seeming ingratitude. 'Why

do you say it like that,' he asked, 'as though you didn't believe me?'

'It's not that,' said Constance, 'I believe you all right. Only when you've got brothers like mine, what you want is a bit of peace. All my life I've had brothers breathing down my neck, watching my every move, checking on who I'm going out with and what time I'm getting home. If I ever got talking to some man in a pub, it was more than his life was worth. My brothers'd be watching his every move, just hoping he'd put a foot wrong so they could jump in and scrag him. It wasn't so much my virtue they were worried about as their own standing in the community. They're very medieval, my brothers. So, what I mean is . . .,' she said after a moment's thoughtful silence, 'it's very nice of you, but I don't need any more bother.'

Memet was silent too: he was more deeply offended than he could permit himself to show. Constance, in a few words, had insulted his dignity, his pride, his sense of exclusiveness, his manhood. He was beginning to get annoyed.

After an unnaturally long pause Constance became aware of this. She had been injudicious. Her worry about his probable infidelity had led her to attack him in an irresponsibly dangerous manner. If she had spoken truthfully and expressed her doubts about his faithfulness, he would have been flattered, gentle and full of mirth. She had felt she'd die rather than give him the satisfaction, but now she'd have to be clever, for by implication she had denigrated his power and his commitment to protect her. Not, she thought, that she needed his or anybody's protection. She had been well able to look after herself since she had been about seven, and, when she came to think about it, she knew herself to be more effective than most men.

While she would not have scored highly in a bout conducted according to the Queensberry Rules, she was strong, agile and quite unscrupulous, since the evenings and holidays of her childhood had been spent in back street and wasteland where enemies, from time immemorial, have come together. But physical victory was a poor thing to a woman and little to preen herself on: any fool could disable another with a judicious cast of fist or foot, a neatly wielded weapon, a dirty trick. Her real power lay in her knowledge of others, her awareness of the weakness of men, the destructive weight of a well-timed laugh. Telling a man the simple truth could reduce him to a wreck, so that, on the whole, she held her punches and her tongue, knowing how deeply she could wound. Now she'd been careless. She had, thought Constance, put her well-shod and shapely right in it, and Memet was cross.

However – 'To be honest,' she said, looking into his set and speechless face, 'it's my brothers I'm a bit worried about.' This was not wholly untrue. She was usually a bit worried about her brothers. Whenever there was something amiss in the district she wondered where her brothers had been at the time, and as she had been making her way to Sainsbury's this thought had yet again crossed her mind.

A few weeks before, her brothers had deposited some things in her kitchen for safe-keeping, and while they were there Barbs had called and had asked, in her friendly and inquisitive fashion, what the cardboard boxes contained. Constance, as was her wont, had paid her little attention, but her brothers had taken fright. 'What's that nosy cow doing here?' they had asked. 'Who does she know? What's her game? Where does she think she gets off, asking questions like that? What's going on? What's occurring?'

Constance had reassured them, or so she hoped: she had

tried to alleviate their suspicions by explaining that Barbs was just like that. She liked to show a matey interest in things, be one of the boys, prove she wasn't stuck-up and so on. They had not seemed wholly convinced but had subsided with mutterings.

Now Constance began to put on an act. She reached out for Memet's hand. He withdrew it. Hell, thought Constance. She said again, 'To be *perfectly* honest, it's not so much Scarlet I'm worried about. It's Barbs . . .'

Memet interrupted. 'Why,' he asked coldly, scarcely moving his lips, 'should you be worried about her?'

'She's missing,' said Constance, watching him closely for signs of shock or sorrow. She found it difficult to speak to him of Barbs, full as she was of jealous suspicion. Try as she might, she couldn't sound normal.

'Why should that worry *you?*' inquired Memet, and for a horrid moment she thought that he was warning her not to speak ill of the love of his life, but he went on: 'She's not a nice woman,' he said.

'I know that,' said Constance, surprised and relieved. 'How do *you* know that?' Memet said nothing but waited, all unawares, for her to continue misleading him. 'So it's my brothers really I'm bothered about – not so much Scarlet, though she is being a bit limp – so it's Barbs I'm *really* worried about.' Here Constance stopped, having confused herself. 'I'll start again,' she said. 'Thing is, Barbs barged in at an inconvenient moment when my brothers were moving some stuff into my place, and they came over all paranoid and looked at her very old-fashioned, and while I *know* they wouldn't do anything to her, now she's gone missing I can't help wondering. See what I mean?' Memet began to look more relaxed, although not completely, and Constance went on, 'So the reason I said all that earlier is because I'm worried about them mostly. What they might've been up to. Because I've had enough of it all my life what with one thing and another, and what I mean is, I don't want you getting yourself into trouble trying to mind my back when I'm OK really, and you'll just land yourself in it doing the unnecessary.' She regretted that she had had to make this incoherent and disingenuous speech, partly because, as she went on, she had begun to listen to what she was saying and had realized that at some level her apprehensions about her family were justified. She was sure – or almost sure – that they had never actually killed anyone, but you could never be quite sure in this world. Could you?

Memet laughed, startling her. 'You're not nearly as clever as you think you are, are you, Connie?' She was so pleased to hear him laugh that she ignored his words and sat on the floor at his feet. 'You thought she was such a nice, kind lady, didn't you? You never took any notice of her. You never knew she was jealous of you, did you?'

'No,' said Connie. 'Was she? Why should she be?'

'Oh, no reason,' said Memet, and he laughed again.

Constance stiffened. She could think of only one reason why Barbs should have been jealous of her, and he was sitting there laughing at her. 'I don't know what you're finding so funny,' she said, and she got up and went into the garden, thinking, as she looked back, that Barbs had always had the ability to put people at odds with each other and, seemingly, was able to do it when she wasn't even there. After a while Memet followed to tell her how much he loved her, but she wouldn't listen.

'This is a funny time to be painting your toenails,' said Scarlet.

'You should never have married again, Mum,' said Camille. She was sitting on her futon, bent over her feet, and
had turned down her stereo because Brian had just marched
in and requested her to do so.

'Oh, Cam,' said Scarlet.

'You should've stayed with my dad,' said Camille.

'You don't know anything about it,' said Scarlet.

'Only because you've never told me,' said Camille. Scarlet stared at her and then blinked. She was slightly drunk
and awkwardly aware of it. 'You never asked me,' she said.

'Oh, Mum,' said Camille, and she sounded suddenly old:
not mature but tired – and old.

Scarlet blinked again: she was projecting her own feelings
on to her child. Her therapist had warned her about this.
'Do you want to talk about it?' she asked.

'No,' said Camille.

'I don't mean now,' said Scarlet, 'I mean tomorrow
maybe. Whenever you like.'

'It's too late,' said Camille. 'You've done it now.'

'But I did it years ago,' said Scarlet, beginning to feel
faintly hysterical. 'It was all when you were a baby.'

'That's what I mean,' said Camille. 'You've ruined my
life, my whole life.' She wondered whether this was going a
bit far and glanced up, surreptitiously, at her mother: her
wasted evening had left her in a bad mood, and she was
determined to take it out on somebody.

'Oh, Cam,' whispered Scarlet, 'don't.'

But Camille had turned back to her toenails and couldn't
see her mother's face. 'You have deprived me of a father's
love,' she said, peering closely at her toes. Scarlet opened her
mouth and hesitated, suspicion kindling within her. 'Damn,'
said Camille, as the brush slipped over on to her flesh.

'*Camille*,' said Scarlet.

'Oh, what?' said Camille, crossly. 'First that silly prat you married comes bursting in here without knocking, and now you've made me paint my feet.'

'Don't talk about your father like that,' said Scarlet.

Camille paused, waiting for a certain new, cold cruelty to resolve itself inside her. It spoke. 'He is not my father,' it said, 'and since you married him I don't think of you as my mother.' She regretted that later. She stayed awake for a long time wondering uneasily whether cruelty was a natural part of her character, or whether its expression was merely an aspect of growing up. She thought she'd better watch it, for if it took control, then no one would ever love her and she would be lonely all through her life. The power of adulthood might not be as much fun as she had imagined. Oh, bugger it, thought Camille.

Her first words the following morning were addressed to Brian, for she was also learning subtlety. 'Brian,' she said, 'I've got to do a project on art and commercialism. Will you help me? I told them in school about you and they said I was ideally positioned.'

'Well, of course,' said Brian. 'I'll make the time,' and the new coldness in Camille noted, through a clear magnifying transparency of ice, that he was pleased to be asked. Camille herself – the Camille whom Camille was used to – merely noted exasperatedly that he seemed to have had plenty of time yesterday, sitting round in the café all morning. A few months before, when she was much younger, she would have screeched this aloud and brought the breakfast table to an uproar, but now she smiled while the coldness took careful and eternal appreciation of the fact that he had been flattered to be asked. Camille, to her own disquiet, was learning the modes of destruction.

'You've got bags under your pretty little eyes, Mum,' she said, in her normal voice. 'I'll wring you out a couple of tea bags.'

'That's kind,' said Scarlet. 'I think I've got a touch of hangover.'

'I'm not surprised,' said Brian, 'not after what you put away last night.'

Once upon a time Camille would have dipped her oar in here: she would have turned on Brian for attacking her mother or chided her mother in no uncertain terms for being a drunken slut. Or, possibly, she would have done a bit of both. As it was, she smiled, rather falsely, for while laughter came naturally to her, smiling, as yet, did not, since only babies and adults can smile with conviction: she realized that her face felt uncomfortable wearing this expression and reverted to her habitual frown.

Scarlet was relieved, since Camille's adolescent smile had reminded her of the expression on the face of some ancient, alien reptile. 'Don't be late home, darling,' she implored.

'I do believe that girl's beginning to grow up,' observed Brian, reaching for the jam as Camille left for the streets. Scarlet said nothing. Another day lay ahead.

By mid-morning she had done what housework she was prepared to do, and although she had used the vacuum cleaner, her nose felt full of dust, her heart heavy: she had picked up all manner of objects – scent bottles, jugs, a Staffordshire dog – wiped them desultorily and put them back. They had lost significance for her yet still had the power to bring her to the verge of tears, reminding her of what they had once meant: of one Easter when the scent had been a gift, of autumn afternoons when she had taken her baby in a pushchair from one to another of the now disappeared junk shops, buying Victorian china, pieces of old lace and old books, looking forward to the future. Now all the pretty things sat around in the present, and all they did was make her regret the past. Sometimes she wished a burglar would come and take them away, but the burglars were interested only in electrical equipment, credit cards and cash. Constance said they were mostly amateurs nowadays.

She went into the garden to call over the wall. 'Constance!' She leaned over the fence to look through the glass of Constance's back door, disappointed to think she might not be there.

'Hang on,' said Constance, emerging into the daylight in the clothes she had worn the night before. 'I just woke up . . .'

'Did I wake you?' asked Scarlet, anxiously.

Constance yawned, considering this question. 'It's a funny thing,' she said, 'but no one ever answers that truthfully. They always say, "Oh no, no," or "I'm glad you did. It was time I got up." They never say, "Yes, you did, you perishing pain in the arse," do they?'

'I *am* sorry,' said Scarlet.

'Don't worry about it,' said Constance. 'It was time I woke up. I was up all night having a row with Memet.'

'What about?' asked Scarlet, who would herself have thought twice before having a row with a Turk. Her mother bracketed Turks with the Portuguese and the Maltese – people you didn't know or, if you did, you didn't cross. Her mother's views, unconventional though they had been, were still highly selective.

'Nothing, really,' said Constance. 'It just blew up out of nothing. One of them – *you* know. I was in a bad mood, and he kept pestering me, so we had words.'

'Poor you,' said Scarlet. 'Did he go home?'

'Not him,' said Constance. 'He's fast asleep in the

bedroom. I slept on the kitchen sofa,' she added, 'and the cat tried to sleep on my face. I had a bad night, really . . .'

'I am sorry,' said Scarlet again, but she knew Constance wasn't angry with her. She never had been. Constance saved all her passion, including rage, for her sexual relationships – which left her calm and useful to her friends. Scarlet had never known her to confuse the issue.

'If I was a few years younger, I'd be a hooker,' said Constance, stretching.

Scarlet protested. 'You wouldn't enjoy it.'

'Am I enjoying this?' demanded Constance, indicating her bedroom window. 'What is this *enjoy* you're always going on about?'

'You know you love it,' said Scarlet, who was referring to Constance's single state and not to her lover.

'I s'pose so,' said Constance, referring to her lover.

'Come and have some coffee,' said Scarlet.

'I'm never going to drink any more coffee,' said Constance. 'It makes me nervous. I'm going on a fast for a few days because everything you eat's bad for you.' She clambered over the fence.

'Do you think we think too much about what we eat?' asked Scarlet, who was beginning to get tired of reading all the labels in the supermarket before buying even a packet of dried beans.

'Of course we do,' said Constance. 'We've got health-conscious. We'll probably all go mad and die fussing over our food. The only worry Mum ever had was getting enough to go round. Ever since they decided sex is good for you and you can't get too much of it, they've thought food's bad for you. There's got to be some reason we all drop dead in the end.'

'What about AIDS?' asked Scarlet.

'That gave the free-lovers a bit of a turn,' admitted Constance, 'but they think if you apply a nice hygienic bit of clingfilm, everything'll be all right. Like not being able to sneeze on the cheese. There's not so much wanking going on as there was, now it's all on offer, so everyone thinks eating saturated fat makes you blind, and they've all got obsessed with what they put in their mouths instead of in their . . .'

'I never seem to talk about anything else but food,' said Scarlet. 'I'm sure I used to talk about other things, but I can't remember what. I'm just a housewife.' Constance said nothing because talk of housework bored her. 'It's worse,' said Scarlet, 'I'm a company wife. I woke up the other morning and I thought, once you married for company, and now you marry the company. You have to do the right things.'

'You aren't half out of date,' said Constance.

'Thanks,' said Scarlet.

'It's not your fault,' said Constance. 'If you was anyone else, I'd say, get divorced, but you did that once and then you went and got married again. You can't help yourself. It's your destiny – all writ up in your stars. You could kill him, I suppose, but you've got to remember this: if you do, what you have to do next is ruffle up your hair and mess up your garments and appear howling and all distressed at your local nick, saying you don't know what came over you. On no account look out your passport and make for the airport because they'll catch you in customs and the judge will be cross and tell you you're a cold-blooded, ruthless and calculating murderess and give you twenty years. If you follow course one, you'll get off with a caution or three months' community work. That's today's Helpful Home Hint.'

'How depressing,' said Scarlet.

'I know,' said Constance, 'but I've got troubles too. My life's no bed of roses.'

'You should sell your jewellery to the big stores,' said Scarlet, not for the first time.

'And get done for VAT?' said Constance. 'You've got to be joking.'

'You wouldn't have to travel about so much. You'd save money that way,' said Scarlet.

'I like travelling about,' said Constance. 'Mostly. Except for the jams on the motorway. I've got a lot of friends round the country, travelling round like I do. I don't want to be stuck in one place, do I?'

'I suppose not,' said Scarlet. She knew that Constance dealt in other, ill-gotten, commodities on these trips but concurred in the popular, criminal view that nicking a lorry-load of underwear was in a different class from stealing wedding rings from old ladies.

Constance frequently reiterated that she would never buy anything that had belonged to somebody else, that meant something to them, that had been warm against their skin or over the fireplace: only brand-new articles, the stuff of commerce in transit between factory and store, the owners of which already had more money than was good for them and were themselves no better than they should be. The rich, Constance held, had got that way by grinding the faces of the poor and taking the tax man for a ride. When Scarlet attempted to disagree, albeit feebly, Constance cited the scandals in the City and pointed out that the gap between the highest- and the lowest-paid was greater now than it had been since the nineteenth century. Money, said Constance, no longer had any relevance to the value of half a dozen eggs or a side of mutton, but had become a separate commodity for rich men to play with. When Scarlet suggested that not all rich men were bad, Constance said that they were, by definition, and would cite Memet's uncles. There was often no arguing with Constance.

'Have you thought any more about Barbs?' asked Scarlet.

'Yes,' said Constance. 'I thought about her.'

'What are you going to do?' asked Scarlet.

'What I was thinking was, why should I do anything?' said Constance.

'I thought you were worried.' Scarlet was still sore that Constance had asked Barbs to mind the cat.

'I was exaggerating,' said Constance. 'If we're going to be absolutely truthful, I don't give a monkey's where she's gone.'

'What if she's lying dead in her bedroom?' asked Scarlet.

'Then *she*'s not going to be worried, is she?' said Constance. 'Lucky old her. No more worries.'

'She's a human being,' said Scarlet.

'So's everybody,' said Constance. 'So what?'

'You know what I mean,' said Scarlet.

'If you watch telly, you'll know there's people lying dead all over the world,' said Constance. 'What's one more, more or less. Anyway, she isn't.'

'Isn't what?' asked Scarlet. 'Isn't a human being, do you mean?'

'Isn't lying dead in her bedroom, I mean,' said Constance. 'You know what I mean. You're just being awkward.'

'You're in a bad mood,' said Scarlet.

'I told you I was,' said Constance.

'I'm curious,' said Scarlet. 'I feel I should be worried, but really I'd just like to know where she is – out of curiosity.'

'I wouldn't waste any sleep,' said Constance. 'Life's too short.'

'Years ago you wouldn't have felt like that,' said Scarlet. 'You were a community, and you all looked after your own.'

'Barbs isn't one of mine,' said Constance. 'She isn't one of yours neither, when you come to think of it. She's American.'

'So only family counts,' said Scarlet.

'And your closest friends,' said Constance. 'All that stuff about community meant you could leave the kids with your mum if you had something to do, and you wouldn't grass on Charlie if the police came looking for him, and you could borrow ten bob to keep you going to the end of the week. But don't run away with the idea it was all Jerusalem the Golden. There were a lot of very nasty people around, then as now, and if one of them turned up in no condition for a party, lying on the towpath, there was no questions asked.' She stopped, wishing that she hadn't said that, as an image of her brothers flickered across her mind.

'But Barbs isn't really a nasty one, not like that,' said Scarlet. 'She means well.'

'I've reverted to type,' said Constance. 'I'm not going to be middle-class any more, with a sense of responsibility. I'm going to mind my own business from now on.' It occurred to Scarlet that Constance's house might be burdened with an embarrassment of cardboard boxes containing knickers or transistors which the police should not be permitted to notice. She was silent. 'I know what you're thinking,' said Constance.

'Then perhaps *I* should say something,' said Scarlet. 'I should go round Holmes Road and make inquiries.'

'*You* don't make inquiries,' said Constance. 'You tell them, and *they* make inquiries.'

'She's a missing person,' said Scarlet.

'No, she's not,' said Constance. 'She's just not there at the moment. Nobody's really a missing person till they're found dead, and then they're not missing any more.'

'I'll ask Brian what he thinks,' said Scarlet, 'when he gets home.'

'I shouldn't think he thinks anything,' said Constance. 'Not about Barbs. Unless . . .'

'Unless what?' asked Scarlet.

'Unless she took time off to mind him instead of the cat,' said Constance.

'You know perfectly well,' said Scarlet, 'that, while Brian may have his faults, faithlessness isn't one of them.'

'Having a fling with Barbs isn't faithlessness,' said Constance, who had been concentrating on this very matter for her own reasons. 'With Barbs it isn't "Stop me and buy one." It's free. She's a women's libber, so it's all on offer. She thinks it makes her more equal.'

'I don't see what difference that makes,' said Scarlet.

'It makes all the difference,' said Constance. 'Faithless is when they fall in love with someone else, not when they're just giving them one.' She had once heard one of her brothers say, 'I've never seen my poor old bird look so tatty.' He had been speaking of his wife, and Constance had been surprised, for this was the language of love and quite unlike the more usual 'Cor, you should've seen the pair she had on 'er.'

'I'm not sure about that,' said Scarlet.

'No, nor am I really,' said Constance. 'But that's what they tell me.'

'Is that what Memet tells you?'

'It's what he's always telling me. That man hasn't got the morals of a ferret. I don't know why I bother with him.' Constance ran her fingers through her hair.

'You love him,' said Scarlet, gloomily. 'You haven't got a hope.'

'Well, I'm not sure about that,' said Constance. 'I could be getting very fed up with him and his little ways. He does unexplained absences and he comes back looking pleased with himself. He says he's had a win somewhere, but when I've been with him he mostly loses. He drinks and gambles and chases women and comes back to me for his dinner.'

'Then why bother with him?' asked Scarlet.

'I like his mind,' said Constance, 'and he's very kind-hearted.'

'I didn't think the Turks were like that,' said Scarlet.

'You don't know them,' said Constance. 'And they've had a bad press. People change. Whole nations change. Look at the Japanese. One minute they're growing bamboos through living prisoners and unravelling their own insides, and the next they've all got their heads down over their computers, making motor cars. And the Germans have calmed down a lot, you've got to admit that. Then look at us. Once upon a time we were all law-abiding citizens, and now we've got football hooligans. My mum wouldn't't've put up with that from any of us. We've all changed. I know some of my brothers were villains, but they dressed well – they wouldn't go out without a wash and a clean shirt and their suits pressed. They didn't make a spectacle of themselves. Not like now. We've got worse.'

'I wonder why?' said Scarlet.

'It's the middle classes,' said Constance. 'They've lost direction, and the working class is taking liberties.'

'I'll never understand your politics,' said Scarlet. 'Not if I live to be a hundred.'

'I haven't got politics,' said Constance, 'just common

sense. Politics don't work. You get one lot with one lot of ideas and they run the country their way, and nobody likes it. Then you get another lot with another lot of ideas and they do it their way, and nobody likes that either. What we want is a dictatorship. I'd start by shooting a few people I know and making them stop digging holes in the road.'

'I'm just going to stop reading the papers at all,' said Scarlet. 'Everything sounds so awful. You think it can't be as bad as all that, and then you turn on the radio and it is. Famine and plague and wars . . .'

'They've changed the Ten Commandments,' said Constance. 'It isn't "Thou shalt not" any more. It's "Thou hast already and, this being the case, thou mightest as well go on doing it, since if thou dothn't, it might be bad for thine psyche, and anyway if we told thee not to, thou wouldst accuse us of being prejudiced and go on doing it all the same." It's a wicked old world,' she concluded.

'My mother used to say it wasn't the world that was wicked but the people in it,' said Scarlet. 'She was always making annoying remarks like that. I don't know where she picked them up.'

'Off her arty pals, I suppose,' said Constance.

Scarlet's mother had moved in the Bohemian world of Chelsea in the years immediately post-war and had acquired the air of insouciant, amoral aristocracy combined with a certain self-righteousness arising from the consciousness of being both aesthetically and (at base) morally correct which had characterized that society at that time. 'She could be maddening,' said Scarlet. 'She still can.'

'She's got style,' Constance said. 'Of a sort.'

'But if you think I'm dated,' said Scarlet, 'what do you think she is?'

'She's gone nearly long enough,' said Constance. 'If you hang around long enough, everything comes back in fashion. Long red fingernails and white clown faces and big black eyes and short hair. Everything!'

'Not ladies in mini-skirts with hats on, I hope,' said Scarlet. 'Not Indian-brave headbands and beads.'

'Maybe not those,' Constance allowed. 'Though beads could be good for business. I could've made a fortune flogging beads to hippies.'

'If you've got some jet,' said Scarlet, 'you could make my mother a necklace and earrings for Christmas. I can't think of anything else to get her.'

'You could get her something to eat,' said Constance. 'When they're very old you might as well give them things to eat. Then, in a manner of speaking, they can take it with them.'

'Drink would be more acceptable,' said Scarlet.

'She still drinking?' asked Constance.

'I have no reason to suppose that she isn't,' said Scarlet.

'Just listen to you,' said Constance. '"I have no reason to suppose that she isn't." Dear, oh dear.'

'I worry about her,' said Scarlet, 'when I've got time. When I'm not worried about something else. I sometimes think she should come and live with us, but I can't impose her on Brian, can I?'

'She can't stand Brian,' said Constance.

'Well, there you are,' said Scarlet, for what Constance stated was undeniable. Scarlet's mother had given it as her opinion that Brian was constipated. 'Do you remember that night?' asked Scarlet.

Her mother had sat at the crowded dinner table, drinking steadily and smoking and speculating aloud on why her daughter had married costive Brian. 'They were all like that in her day. They thought they could say anything and get away with it.'

'I expect they thought it was cute,' said Constance.

'They did,' said Scarlet, 'and clever, and nobody was supposed to have any inhibitions. It was terribly embarrassing for a child. I used to go and hide all the time.'

'Mind you,' said Constance, 'the new generation's a bit like that. The things they say . . .'

'I know,' said Scarlet. 'Camille's much more like my mother than she is me. I don't know how it happened.'

'Genes, I s'pose,' said Constance. 'Bloody things. I like your mother, though. She isn't boring.'

'No,' Scarlet agreed. 'She isn't boring, but she can be awfully tiresome. I wish I knew what I should do with her. I suppose in the old days, if we'd been like you, she'd have been living with us as a matter of course.'

'Not necessarily,' said Constance. 'Not your mum. There were limits. Some of the old girls drank, but they knew when to keep their mouths shut. Your mother's outrageous.'

'I wish I knew she was happy,' said Scarlet.

'There you go again,' said Constance. 'You're always on about *happy* and *enjoy*. Memet's the same. Thinks about nothing but having a good time.'

'I'm not like that,' said Scarlet.

'No, but you go on about it. It means you're deeply insecure somewhere.'

'That's probably why I have to see a therapist,' said Scarlet humbly.

'You don't really have to see a therapist at all. You just do it to upset Brian,' said Constance.

'No, I don't,' said Scarlet.

'Then maybe you do it to upset your mum. It's a bit

like committing suicide, seeing a psychiatrist. Makes every-one else feel guilty.'

'You,' said Scarlet, 'sometimes *remind* me of my mum.'

'We are not dissimilar,' said Constance, lightly, 'both being artistic and free of bourgeois values.'

'My mother isn't artistic,' said Scarlet. 'She just knocked around with artists. She says herself she's an artist's moll – or she was.'

'It rubs off,' said Constance. 'All those models carried on the same way the artists did. You only have to read a book about the Left Bank.'

'I don't read as much as you,' said Scarlet.

'You should go down the High Street,' said Constance. 'You'd be amazed what you can pick up on the remainder counter for a song.'

'We've got no room for any more books,' said Scarlet. 'The shelves are full.'

'They say you can tell all about a person from looking at his books,' said Constance, who had become addicted to book-collecting since she had acquired a car-load of second-hand volumes from a fair in the Midlands. She had originally intended to resell them but found she had grown attached to them and had built shelves in her sitting-room. They lay, opened and half read, all over her house.

'I don't know what they'd make of ours,' said Scarlet. 'Brian only buys novels by those men, and I haven't bought a book for years – not since Elizabeth David, I don't think.'

'I can't read books by men,' said Constance. 'They will go on about their willies and chopping blondes to bits, and who cares?'

'I think they think we do,' said Scarlet.

'I don't think they do,' said Constance. 'I think they just can't really think about anything else.'

'How depressing,' said Scarlet. This phrase was becoming habitual with her.

'People like Barbs encourage them,' said Constance. 'She pretends she thinks they're wonderful.'

'I wonder where she is?' said Scarlet.

'She'll be do-gooding somewhere,' said Constance. 'You can put money on it. She's probably enticed a man with a beard and a lot of snotty children away from his wife, and she'll be shacked up with them in a mobile home on the outskirts of Llangollen, cooking beans and magic mushrooms and playing the flute and moaning about the artificial restrictions of society.'

'How do you know?' asked Scarlet. 'You said you had no idea where she'd gone.'

'I'm guessing,' said Constance. 'She's done it before. She went off to Norfolk with the plumber and his other girl-friend and her stepkids, and it didn't work. She asked me to go too.'

'How frightful,' said Scarlet.

'She's always doing it,' said Constance.

When she had gone Scarlet thought how bored with their conversation Brian would have been had he been present, and then she thought that, with him around, they wouldn't have had that conversation and *she* would have been bored. Connie held that it was a simple matter to forgive your enemies because, if you had the sense you were born with, you didn't see much of them, whereas with the way society was constituted, you spent most of your time with your nearest and dearest, and the things they could do to annoy you made the whole concept of forgiveness extremely difficult to entertain.

'But I don't believe in God,' said Sam, lighting a cigarette.

65

'Shut up or he'll hear you,' said Camille. 'Connie says she wonders a bit about the sort of God who could make the human race and *love* it. She says her brother had a mate who kept ferrets and they were nasty, ugly, vicious little bastards, and he adored them. And Connie's *religious.*'

'So why's she going round with a Muslim?' demanded Sam.

'He's religious too,' explained Camille.

'So why'd she say that thing about ferrets?' inquired Sam further.

'I dunno,' said Camille, 'I expect she was making a what-d'you-call-it? – one of those things.'

'A simile?' said Sam.

'Something like that,' said Camille. 'Anyway, it can't do any harm to pray, can it?'

'It might,' said Sam. 'Like taking antibiotics when you don't need them. They say you shouldn't do that. Besides, I don't think you're supposed to pray for people to leave their girlfriends and fall in love with you.'

'Well, you'll just have to seduce him all by yourself,' said Camille, reasonably. 'Get him a bit drunk, and wear a suspender belt, and make your mouth go like this . . .' She dropped her lower lip in a pout.

'When you make your mouth go like that,' said Sam, 'it looks like a baboon's bottom. *And* you don't half look stupid.'

'It's supposed to be very sexy,' said Camille. 'They always tell models to do it.'

'That's probably why they always look stupid,' said Sam. 'It's how they probably got their reputation for being thick.'

'*I'm* going to be a model,' said Camille. 'Don't say it,' she added.

'You got most of the qualifications,' said Sam. 'Dumb, face like a monkey's bum . . .'

'I gave you that one,' said Camille. 'It's not fair.'

'You should be more careful,' said Sam. 'Shall I ask him out to dinner?'

'You've got no money,' said Camille.

'I could ask him home,' said Sam. 'I could ask him and Tim and you, and make my mum go out for the evening.'

'That doesn't work,' Camille reminded her. 'Something always goes wrong.'

'Yes, but we're older now,' said Sam.

'They don't think so,' said Camille. 'You're much more sensible than you used to be, but your mum can't see it, and my mum still thinks I'm three and a half.'

'We could ask Barbs,' said Sam. 'She'd let us have it at her place.'

'No, we couldn't,' said Camille. 'She's disappeared.'

'What d'you mean, disappeared?' asked Sam. 'Where's she gone?'

'Nobody knows,' said Camille. 'She's just not there, and nobody knows where she is. Mum and Connie keep talking about it, but they don't do anything. I don't think they care much really.'

'But that's awful,' said Sam, virtuously. 'Something might have happened to her.'

'That's what Mum says. And Con says, if it has, there's nothing they can do about it. They're always going on about it, though. It's getting boring.'

'But why don't they do something?'

'Con doesn't want to get mixed up in anything,' explained Camille. 'I don't think her affairs would bear . . . whats-it?'

'Exposure?' offered Sam.

'Exposure,' agreed Camille. 'She doesn't want people nosing round. I can see her point.'

'Maybe *we* should tell the police,' suggested Sam, 'if *they* won't.' Here she was prompted less by social conscience than by a delight in drama.

'You want to get mixed up with them?' asked Camille.

'No, maybe not,' said Sam. 'Tell you what, though, we could get in her house and have a look round . . .'

'And,' cried Camille, 'we could . . .'

'. . . have a party there,' concluded Sam.

They discussed for a moment the possibility that they might get into dreadful trouble but discounted it. As they said, Barbs wouldn't mind. Particularly not if she was dead.

'Will you ask *him* for me?' said Sam.

'No, I won't,' said Camille. 'You're a big girl now. Ask him yourself.'

'What shall I say?' asked Sam.

'Say, "I think you're the most gorgeous thing I've ever seen, come to my arms at once . . ." No. Just say, "I'm having a few friends round to dinner. Would you like to come too?" Simple.'

'It sounds a bit stupid,' said Sam.

'Then how else would you put it?' asked Camille. 'How would your mum put it, for instance?'

'She'd send out an invitation,' said Sam. 'Maybe I should do that. One of those At Home cards.'

'At Barbs's home?' said Camille. 'How'd you get in?'

'Break a window,' said Sam. 'Tim's been doing wood-work. He could mend it next day.'

'That would work in theory,' said Camille carefully, 'but not in practice.'

'Why not?' demanded Sam.

'You know why not,' said Camille. 'He might say he'd

do it, but he wouldn't. He's lazy and unreliable. It's his age.'

'You're just being awkward,' said Sam. 'Just making difficulties, that's all.' She found her own ascent to maturity impeded by her friend's unexpected display of common sense. 'Where's your adventurous spirit?'

'I haven't got an adventurous spirit,' said Camille. 'I'm a coward except when I'm drunk.'

'No, you're not,' said Sam.

'Yes, I am,' said Camille, and they embarked on one of the pointless quarrels which had characterized their relationship since they had learned to speak.

'It's about time we asked Pam to dinner,' said Scarlet one evening.

'Why?' asked Brian. This had become an automatic response to most of his wife's suggestions, and Scarlet had learned to have a few answers ready.

'Because we haven't seen her since her barbecue,' she said.

'We haven't seen the Queen since the garden party,' said Brian, 'but I don't suppose you'll be asking her to dinner.' He was in a good frame of mind: he often referred to the royal garden party when he was in a good frame of mind. Scarlet still found the episode entirely mysterious, since she could think of no reason at all why they had been invited. It was improbable in the extreme that Brian's sterling qualities had come to the notice of the Comptroller of the Household, and she could only assume that the summons had been the consequence of her father's having been an RA. Unless, of course, there had been a muddle in the names. That sort of thing happened more often than was realized. Naturally, she had never mentioned these doubts to Brian.

'She's been lonely since Danny went,' said Scarlet. 'It's lonely for her, especially now Sam's growing up.' Sam had been responsible for the departure of her mother's lover, but Pam had not complained openly, since it put all of them in a bad light: her lover had been revealed as pusillanimous, Sam as a harridan and herself as a person of no control or strength of will.

'That girl's a bad influence on Camille,' said Brian. 'She's badly brought-up.'

Scarlet turned away uneasily at the mention of upbringing: Brian's first wife had telephoned only a few weeks before to say that Brian's son was causing her hair to turn grey and fall out. She had not wanted to speak to Brian, but she had to speak to somebody, and she knew Scarlet would understand. Scarlet had understood that she was meant to understand that Brian was a hopeless father and a worthless human being, and she had not told him of the call. Sometimes she thought of her first husband and wondered briefly whether gross infidelity was really sufficient cause for divorce and whether faithless men were not perhaps – overall – more amusing than the other sort. She had somehow found it difficult to defend Brian against the accusations of his first wife, who held that he was inept and ineffectual in the field of human relationships. Fortunately, she was a feminist and seldom asked for extra money, since she would consider that degrading, although she had accepted a house and school fees. Scarlet had found it all very puzzling and upsetting: she couldn't envisage herself telephoning her first husband's second wife to complain about her child – even if they hadn't gone to Australia. She wondered for a moment whether he had stopped being unfaithful.

'You're miles away,' said Brian.

'What?' said Scarlet.

'I said I'd seen Sam hanging about on the towpath with a bunch of yobs.'

'They're probably all Westminster boys,' said Scarlet. 'Most of their friends are.' Later she wondered what Brian had been doing on the towpath, forgetting that his favourite restaurant commanded a view of the canal.

'What's for dinner?' Brian inquired.

'Chicken,' said Scarlet. 'I think I'll ask Pam next week.'

'It's always chicken,' said Brian. 'I'll be growing feathers soon.'

'White meat,' said Scarlet. 'It hasn't got so much cholesterol . . .' But Brian was not really angry, only teasing. 'We'll have fish tomorrow,' said Scarlet, who had got into the habit of ceaseless apology. She went half-way upstairs and called, 'Camille!'

'Wot?' demanded Camille, peering down over the banister rail.

'You should say, "What is it, dearest Mama?"' said Scarlet, gaily.

Camille didn't smile. 'So, OK. Say I've said that. What next?'

'Dinner,' said Scarlet, flatly.

'How's the project going?' asked Brian, drawing up his chair. Scarlet and Camille looked blank. 'Art and commercialism,' he prompted.

'All right,' said Camille, after a moment's pause for recollection.

Scarlet tensed: please, she said silently, please talk about it, beloved Camille. Please ask his advice and then go and get your books, and let's behave like a normal family.

But she looked back to her own childhood and wondered

71

where she had got the idea that she knew what a normal family would be like. Her parents had never really *lived* anywhere: they had inhabited studios and cottages and areas of other people's houses and spent all their leisure time, which had been considerable, in pubs with other flamboyant artists and a few bitter intellectuals who were endlessly aggrieved at the turn the world was taking. She had been left outside a great many pubs on warm summer evenings while models and some younger aspiring painters had occasionally checked to see if she was still there. Sometimes they had speculated on how she would develop but not often: mostly she was taken for granted because she had been such a quiet child, sitting dozily in her pram outside the Dog and Duck while the sun went down. It had been a deep and tub-like pram, and they had used it to convey her from place to place long after she had been of an age to be confined in such a vehicle. It was convenient because they could put her to sleep in it when they stayed overnight in strange houses.

As she grew older her school friends – of whom there were a great many, since she was forced to change schools almost yearly as her parents flitted – sometimes expressed envy at her adventurous lifestyle. This had served to console her a little and relieve the vicarious shame that her parents inspired in her: they were so *silly*.

Once she had tried to describe these feelings to Brian, but, while he had been prepared to admit that her mother was virtually certifiable, he had given it as his opinion that her father had been a remarkable man and a fine artist and richly entitled to his eccentricities: indeed, it had been incumbent on him, Brian had implied, to flout the conventions. Scarlet had nearly despaired. She had divorced her first husband because he showed signs of becoming like her father, and now, at her second attempt, the man she had married, while not apparently planning to emulate her parent, yet found him admirable. Her therapist had, naturally, put it to her that she had married her first husband just *because* he resembled her father, but Scarlet had rejected the suggestion quite emphatically: he had been a quiet, timorous boy until he discovered the excitement of chasing women, and he had not been artistic at all.

'It should be easy for you,' remarked Brian, addressing his stepdaughter in what Scarlet felt to be an ill-advised tone of patronage, 'with your grandfather's reputation and my experience.'

'They don't know about my grandfather,' said Camille. 'Anyway he's out of fashion. He'll have to be dead a bit longer before he comes back.' She was unimpressed by both her grandfather's reputation and his work: she had removed from her bedroom wall a large still-life of gladioli and a small representation of a baby's head and stacked them carelessly on the landing in order to make room for a poster of Humphrey Bogart. Scarlet had been irrationally annoyed with her.

Brian chewed a bit of chicken and looked as though he was about to speak, so Camille spoke again. 'I wonder what's happened to Barbs?' she surmised, changing the subject.

'Why should anything have happened to her?' asked Brian.

'She's not there,' said Camille. 'She's disappeared.'

'What do you mean, disappeared?' pressed Brian, spearing a noodle.

'Gone,' said Camille. 'Not there.'

'Gone is one thing,' said Brian. 'Gone on holiday, gone out for a walk . . .'

73

'Gone mad,' interrupted Camille helpfully.

'*Disappeared*,' continued Brian, 'has quite different conno-
tations. It's a legal term . . .'

'No, it isn't,' interrupted Camille again.

Scarlet said, 'Does anyone want any more chicken?'

'*Disappeared*,' said Brian, 'tends to mean that something
bad, even something criminal, has occurred.'

Scarlet, who agreed with him, wished that he were
better able to express himself. She didn't know how to
clarify and quantify her anxieties, and she wished that her
husband could do so for her without revealing his paucity
of intellect. She wished that she could rely on him and
wondered where she had acquired such unrealistic expecta-
tions. Nothing in her life had led her to suppose that men
could be relied on any more than anyone else. It must, she
thought, have been something she read.

'Anyway,' said Camille, 'she's not there, and nobody
knows where she is.'

'Why do you say that?' asked Brian. 'Probably plenty of
people know where she is. She's probably on holiday with a
lot of people, having a good time.'

'You know what I mean,' said Camille. '*We* don't know
where she is.'

'Why should you?' said Brian. 'Are you your brother's
keeper?'

'I don't actually care where she is,' said Camille, beginning to lose her fragile temper, 'but Mum does, or at least
she *says* she does – she cares about everyone, don't you,
Mum? Don't you care about everyone?'

'You're making me sound like Barbs,' protested Scarlet.
'I'm not like that.'

Camille was not yet sufficiently enraged to contradict
her. Instead she sat and considered the matter. 'No,' she

agreed after a while. 'You're not as bad as Barbs, but you are a bit wet.'

'Don't talk to your mother like that,' said Brian, merely because he felt that he should.

'It's all right,' said Scarlet, thinking that if that was all Camille accused her of, she would have few worries. 'I *am* wet,' she added, involuntarily.

Brian did not say anything for a moment. He would not, himself, have remarked upon it, but his wife undoubtedly lacked backbone. None the less, civilized people should not be called upon to suffer such cheek from the younger generation, who had little spending power and did nothing to justify their existence. 'There's no need to be rude,' he said in as mild a tone as he could muster.

'Yes, there is,' said Camille. 'What would have happened to the world if Churchill had been too scared to be rude to Hitler when he marched into Sarajevo?'

'That wasn't Hitler,' said Scarlet, aghast at the depths of ignorance her child so often revealed.

'Don't they teach you anything at that school?' inquired Brian, not without some satisfaction at what must be the child's discomfiture.

'No, not really,' said Camille, showing no signs of discomfiture whatever.

Scarlet relaxed a little: a mine had been skirted. Until recently, Camille would have responded to a rebuke with a display of bestial ferocity. She had clearly been about to lose her temper but had controlled herself.

'You should've sent me to a decent school,' said Camille. 'You better send me to a tutorial college before I'm too old.'

'They're a con,' said Brian, 'a complete waste of money.'

'You got plenty,' said Camille. 'Or did the bottom drop out of advertising?'

'*Camille?*' said Scarlet.

They were both frightened of her, Camille noted with bitter delight: afraid she'd upset one of them so that the other would have to intervene before the family dinner broke up with a crash of plates and a splash of blazing gravy. 'Doesn't matter anyway,' she said. 'I'm going to be a kennel-maid.'

'Oh, really?' said Brian.

'Yeah,' said Camille, 'and then I'm going to train.'

'What training do you need to be a kennel-maid?' inquired Brian.

'I'm going to be a trainer,' explained Camille.

'Oh, Camille,' said Scarlet.

'In between modelling,' said Camille.

'What happened to law and medicine?' asked Brian, rolling his eyes and grinning sourly. 'Why not be a barrister or a doctor?'

'I haven't got the education,' said Camille. 'I suppose I could go in for advertising.'

Scarlet thought that, if her mother were here, she would now have cried, 'Game, set and match,' and uttered a throaty laugh. She herself felt like a fair-minded vegetarian at a bullfight, filled with both alarm for the bull and reluctant admiration for the matador, who seems, on the face of it, to be at a disadvantage.

'But you're so clever, Camille,' she said. 'Why throw your life away?'

'Connie's brother,' said Camille, 'has got kennels down Hackney dog track, a house twice the size of this in Chigwell and a villa in Spain, and he knows people in Walthamstow who sent all their sons to public school, so they got educated.'

'Oh, *Connie*,' said Brian, as one who expected as much: he

wanted to say that these characters of whom his step-daughter spoke contributed nothing valuable to society, but was unprepared to defend the ethics and value of advertising in a market economy to a girl who was incapable of grasping the subtleties of an argument.

'And Connie,' pursued Camille, 'lives in a house the same as this and she never had to work for it.'

'And what about the drop-outs?' asked Brian. 'What if you end up like them?'

'I'm not going to end up like them,' said Camille. 'I'll sell Grandpa's pictures when his reputation comes round.'

She realized she had missed an opportunity to needle Brian and went on, 'Tim says drop-outs are the fault of a cynical and uncompassionate administration who're buggered if they're going to waste good money on a load of lunatics, so they've slung them out and turned the asylums into conference centres for advertising agencies.'

'Oh, *Tim*,' sighed Scarlet, but she thought the sentiments sounded more like Constance's.

'The government's mad,' concluded Camille, 'and the rest of the country's caught it. It happens like that some-times.'

'Who told you that?' asked Brian. Camille thought his smile made him look like one of Mick's greyhounds.

'Nobody told me,' she said. 'I can see it for myself. It's obvious.'

'Not to me,' said Brian.

Dear Lord, he can be stupid, thought Scarlet, as she saw Camille about to respond with the surprised gratification of a matador to whom the bull has blindly turned his flank. 'That's all beside the point,' she said hurriedly. 'What about your homework? We were talking about your proj-ect.'

'*You* were,' corrected Camille. '*I* was talking about Barbs.'

'Oh, damn Barbs,' said her mother, exasperatedly. 'Who cares about Barbs?'

'I thought you did,' said Camille.

'Well, I do,' said Scarlet, 'only what can I do about her?'

'That's what the government says,' said Camille. 'What's for pudding?'

'Yoghurt and honey,' said Scarlet.

'Yuk,' said Camille. 'I'm going to watch telly.'

'What about your homework?' cried Scarlet.

'Do it later,' said Camille.

When, wondered Scarlet, drearily, would she ever learn not to hope, not to believe her daughter when she expressed interest in some aspect of her school work? She remembered the dozens and dozens of exercise books with two or three pages written on and the rest left virgin, the textbooks defaced by doodles, the *waste*. No wonder the education system was bankrupt. 'They don't seem to teach them *anything*,' she said.

'Perhaps we should send her to a tutorial college,' said Brian, unexpectedly. He had looked at his wife's unguarded face and forgotten for a moment that life was a deadly game in which you had to keep your cards close to your chest and your back to the wall, your eyes open and your nose clean in order not to end up in the gutter with your hat in your hand. Brian lived with a primitive terror of outer darkness which he rationalized as a fear of failure: this he further refined into a disinclination to live out of London. If, he reasoned, you couldn't live in a fashionable district with a BMW in a parking spot you had paid for, then you might as well not live at all. But that look of defeat on his wife's face was conducive neither to his sense of success nor to his peace of mind. It would do him no harm if it was known that his stepdaughter was attending a reputable and expensive crammer.

'Can we afford it?' asked Scarlet, forgetting on the instant her vow to abandon the practice of hope.

'We'll find the money somehow,' said Brian.

'I *love* you,' said Scarlet, illuminated by the transient high of mistaken anticipation.

'It's important for a girl to have a proper career,' said Brian. 'Mindless women are no good to anyone – not themselves, their husbands or their children.' Scarlet thought first that this sentiment could be attributable to Barbs, then that, in view of her own lack of a career, it was insensitive of Brian to mention it and then that he had said it out of spite. She decided she didn't love him much after all.

Constance sat threading beads, old beads of Venetian glass, which fell with a faint, decisive click, each upon the other, glittering in the light from her Anglepoise lamp. It was monotonous, soothing work, and she was half tranced in the warm, heavy evening. One, two, three, she said silently to the succession of gleaming globes. One, two, three, and her thoughts gathered unobtrusively above her counting. Her thoughts were growing darker: occasionally one would cause her heart to quicken its beat and then quieten again. Of all her lovers, she told herself, Memet was the least worthy, the most faithless, a liar and a layabout and not the kind her mother would have approved of. He had probably told her a lie of one sort or another every time they met. He couldn't keep his hands off women, and most likely, under his brown flawless skin, he was riddled with disease – disease he had caught from the soft, unwholesome flesh of nameless women. One, two, three . . . 'Anything that moves,' her brothers had said. 'He'd screw anything that moves.'

'You can't talk,' she had said. 'You lily-white lot.'

'But you're our sister,' they'd said. 'No one's going to upset our sister and get away with it.' She had demanded then whether she *looked* upset, and they'd had to agree that she looked calm enough. 'Probably all those pills and potions,' they'd said. 'All that health food's turned you into a zombie.' They had seen her lover, not once but many times, in the pubs and the clubs, chatting up girls.

'You're a dirty-minded bunch of troublemakers,' she had told them. 'He's richer than you and smarter than you, and you're jealous.' Her thoughts gathered and broke at the memory. She threw down the beads, and a few rolled on to the floor. Carefully she knelt and gathered them up. Jealous, she thought, jealous. One, two, three . . . She wasn't getting any younger. It was no fun loving a person like Memet, especially when he wouldn't commit himself to her in a civilized and law-abiding manner. She thought that once she would have been described as an 'old maid' and wondered whether she could blame her brothers or if it was all her own fault for being too easy-going. Unlike some she could mention, she had never claimed to have stayed unmarried out of any particular principle. It had just happened that way.

'Connie.'

'Oh,' she cried, 'what the hell d'you think you're doing, creeping up on me like that? You frightened the shit out of me.'

'I'm sorry,' said Scarlet. 'I've got no shoes on – it was so hot. What are you doing down there?'

'What do I look as though I'm doing?' demanded Connie.

'I'm drinking the cat's milk, of course. I always do that of an evening. You ask some stupid questions, don't you?'

'I *am* stupid,' said Scarlet. 'Everyone keeps saying so. It's all I hear. Stupid, stupid, stupid.'

Connie scrambled up, meeting some resistance from her long skirt. 'What's wrong with you?' she asked.

'Oh, nothing,' said Scarlet. 'I'm just sick of everything.'

'Join the club,' said Connie, but she was glad to see her weak and neurotic neighbour. Never, she swore, never would she let life mess her around the way it had messed Scarlet. 'Tell Connie all about it,' she invited, relieved to have, for a time, someone other than Memet upon whom to focus her attention, someone more miserable than herself and more . . . 'You're not stupid,' she said. 'You just don't see things straight.'

'But I think I do,' said Scarlet. 'I think that's the trouble. Everyone thinks I don't and I *do*.'

'Yes, well, everyone thinks that way,' said Constance. 'Lunatics, prime ministers, they all think the same way. Only *they* know what's really going on.'

'I don't know what's going on,' said Scarlet. 'I just know something is. I've got a feeling.'

'Nasty things, feelings,' said Constance. 'You don't want to have too many of them. Have a drink.'

'I don't think I could face any more peppermint or camomile,' said Scarlet, frankly.

'I said a *drink*,' said Constance, opening the cupboard over the draining board. 'Unless Genghis Khan's had the lot. He has too, the little bastard,' she added, after a short, vain, search in the corners. 'We'll have to go down the off-licence.'

'I've got no shoes on,' said Scarlet.

'So go and get some,' said Constance. 'Hop over the fence and find your footwear. OK?'

There was the scent of freshly cut privet in the street, and Constance pulled a handful of petals from a neighbour's falling rose as she passed. 'Positively idyllic,' she observed. She stopped at Barbs's house and pushed open the gate. 'Come and have a look,' she said.

'What at?' asked Scarlet.

'*I* don't know,' said Constance, 'scene of the crime, I suppose.'

'You don't know there's been a crime,' said Scarlet. 'There hasn't been a crime. We'd have heard. If she was dead in there, there'd be flies – and rats.'

'You're disgusting,' said Constance, making her way down the narrow path at the side of the house.

'No, really,' said Scarlet, following her reluctantly. If you were sure there was no one at home, then creeping round a person's house felt like trespass.

'They wouldn't be swarming all over Kentish Town, would they, those rats and flies?' demanded Constance, opening the tall wooden gate to the back garden. 'Silly bitch should keep this locked,' she said. 'Not that they're not already,' she added to her previous remark. 'I mean, do you think they'd be nestling all over the roof like a tea-cosy? You're thinking of vultures. If there was flies and rats over every dead thing round here, we'd have a bigger problem than what we've got.'

They were standing on the paved area behind the house: all the windows were dark, the garden chairs and the round table abandoned and vulnerable.

'See,' said Constance, 'she's left the furniture out.'

'She always does,' said Scarlet. 'We all do.'

'Not when we're going away, we don't', said Constance. 'When we're going away – when we *know* we're going away – we stack it in the kitchen, don't we?'

'I suppose so,' said Scarlet, 'but the weather's been so fine . . .'

'It's not a spot of rain we've got to worry about,' said Constance, 'it's robbers. It's no good nailing things down these days. They just take the patio too.'

'We're being silly,' said Scarlet. 'We're over-dramatizing. We didn't know her so well as we think. She must have had a life apart from what we know about and she's – living it,' she concluded, lamely.

'You're talking about her as though she was dead,' said Constance. 'In a way you're right, I suppose. If she's dead somewhere else, it's got nothing to do with us, but if she's dead on our doorstep, we ought to do something.'

'You sound as though disasters on the other side of the world shouldn't concern us at all,' said Scarlet.

'That's right,' said Constance. 'Don't start talking like her or I'll think her spirit's got into you.'

Scarlet went to look through the glass doors, wondering about the relationship between distance and responsibility. It was true that she worried more about her mother now she was living near by than she had when she was living in the Tuscan hills, but that might only be because of the possibility that she would call without warning. 'There's no point in hanging round here,' she said. 'I suggest we wait a day or two and then think again.'

'Don't you sound *sensible?*' said Constance. 'OK.' She closed the wooden gate and pushed a brick against it with her foot. 'If she had half an ounce of sense,' she said, 'she'd've put a lock on this thing.'

'When you were a child,' said Scarlet, 'nobody bothered locking their doors round here.'

Constance patted her shoulder indulgently. She had seldom lied to her friend, but she knew that she could have described to her a proletarian custom whereby retired coal-men ate live eel-worms and not have been disbelieved. Whereas once the working class might have looked to the middle classes for an example of probity and upright behaviour, now the middle classes looked to the working class as the custodians of vanishing tradition and folk culture. That, at any rate, was her experience, living where she did: in other districts, she was aware, things were probably different. Here the élite rolled up their louvred or holland blinds to stick Labour Party posters on their window panes when elections came round. Her mum would never had done anything so untidy or indiscreet, and she'd been a Tory all her life.

The off-licence was empty except for two drop-outs buying canned beer: the proprietor contrived to address Scarlet and Constance without once taking his eyes off his other customers, not even as he wrapped a bottle of Smirnoff and extracted six cans of Long Life from under the glass counter. Only as the men left did he relax sufficiently to give Constance a glance of bitter complicity and move his lips soundlessly. He seemed to take for granted that she would share his views on the derelicts.

Outside a mad woman was talking to herself: she wore several coats and had a troubled, concentrated expression. Passers-by gave her a wide berth. As they walked away Scarlet observed another woman bearing down on the many-coated one with the air of a person about to commit good works. For a second she thought that the lost one was lost no more and Barbs was back on the beat, but then she saw that the women were about to share a can of something and were clearly old mates.

'Hogarthian, isn't it?' said Constance.

'Let's get back,' said Scarlet. 'I must feed Camille.'

Passing Barbs's house yet again, Constance stopped. 'The gate's open,' she said, 'and I wedged it with a brick.'

'Oh, never mind,' said Scarlet. 'Do let's get back.'

'Hang on,' said Constance, venturing cautiously up the path. She pushed the gate further open and peered round in the twilight. 'Come out, come out, whoever you are,' she yelled.

'Connie,' implored Scarlet from the street. 'Everyone'll hear you.'

'So what?' said Constance, returning. 'I'm being a good citizen.'

'You're disturbing the peace,' said Scarlet. 'You nearly woke the dead.' She thought of the local cemetery: if they all woke up, they'd come round demanding their houses back; they'd have to be sheltered and fed and appeased with promises. They'd put a terrible strain on the council: if they *all* wakened up, right down through the layers of time, there'd be cavemen mouthing mindless questions in the barren, gameless desert of streets and traffic, and it would be the end of the world. Or it might be that she would have to barricade the windows against the revenants, against all the figures from the history books who had once had a lease on life and property and wanted their rights back. She thought that her therapist would say that this was yet another example of her low self-esteem, a manifestation of her feeling that she herself was undeserving of both property and life. She thought that as she knew so well what her therapist would say, it was indeed a waste of money to continue seeing her. It was not that her therapist was possessed of unusual wisdom or insight and that Scarlet had learned from her: it was just that Scarlet had discerned her way of thought and her approach to the problems which beset the insecure and so found her entirely predictable. Looking to her for comfort was like looking through a drawer for something which you knew was not there because you had looked so often before: you knew what *was* there – in painful and tedious detail – but there was nothing that you wanted.

'Oh, God, I'm depressed,' said Scarlet.

'Tell me about it,' said Constance, sardonically, as they reached her house.

'There doesn't seem any point in anything,' said Scarlet. 'You get up, you go round, you go to bed. Why?'

'Search me,' said Constance, unlocking her front door. 'Go down the kitchen and find a couple of glasses. You'll feel better in a min.'

'I'm just going to go over the fence and see what Camille's doing,' said Scarlet, loath to say what she really meant – that she wanted to make sure Camille was all right – because that would imply that she might not be. 'Camo,' she called from her own kitchen.

'Yeah,' said Camille from the sitting-room and Scarlet felt happier: all that she loved in the world was safely indoors, not roaming the streets with the dispossessed, the vengeful, the undead.

'Come round to Connie's,' she said. 'Bring a Coke.'

'I'm watching telly,' said Camille.

'You can watch it at Connie's,' said Scarlet. 'Come on.'

And to her surprise, Camille did.

'May as well sit in the garden,' said Constance, 'breathe in the traffic fumes.' But her garden smelled of honeysuckle and jasmine and roses from the bushes which grew where once the hens had scratched.

'I suppose that bit of garden must be well manured,' said Scarlet, idly sipping vodka and tonic.

'It's OK now,' said Constance, who knew about these

things. 'Chicken shit burns plants up if it's not well rotted.'

'How sweet,' said Camille. 'What about dog shit?'

'No good,' said Constance. 'The body waste of carnivores is no good to the earth.'

'Pity,' said Camille. 'I was thinking Mick could sell the muck from the kennels as a sideline.'

'Don't think he needs one,' said Constance. 'Mick's doing very nicely, all things considered. Had a bit of bad luck but it passes. Like life, really.'

Scarlet wondered whether now was the moment to delve further into Camille's ambitions. 'Did you tell Connie you were going to be a kennel-maid?' she asked.

'What's that?' said Connie.

'Oh, shut up, Mum,' said Camille.

'Have you changed your mind?' asked Scarlet, upon whom vodka was having its initial, soothing effect.

'I hadn't made my mind *up*,' said Camille. 'I was just *thinking*.'

'Oh,' said Scarlet, nodding wisely.

'I think I missed something,' said Constance.

'I was going to be a kennel-maid,' said Camille, 'only I hadn't quite decided.' She didn't mention training in case Connie found her presumptuous.

'Come off it,' said Constance. 'You couldn't stand it for a second.'

'Yes, I could,' said Camille. 'I'd love it.'

'How long since you've been down the kennels?' asked Constance. 'You got any idea what it's like?'

'How long since you took me?' asked Camille. 'I was ten or twelve . . .'

'You were that at the most,' said Constance. 'More like five or six.'

'Well, I remember it perfectly,' said Camille. 'It was lovely.'

'I'll take you again if you like,' offered Constance. 'You can refresh your memory. It'll be like the old days.'

'You haven't got time . . .,' began Scarlet.

'When?' demanded Camille.

'I've got to go soon,' said Constance. 'It's my niece's birthday soon. Maybe we'll go Monday.'

'After school,' said Scarlet automatically.

'Monday doesn't matter,' said Camille. 'We never do a thing on Monday. We can go any time.'

Scarlet didn't argue as she might have done if she hadn't had a large vodka. Just at present it didn't seem to matter if Camille missed a day of school. 'Where's Memet?' she asked. 'Is he coming round?' She hoped he wasn't, for he always seemed to talk about himself and kept Connie largely silent, which meant that no one else present had any amusement at all. All men were the same, of course: they all liked to hold the floor while the womenfolk listened respectfully, but then you'd think a Turk would be more interesting. On the other hand, Memet had been to public school, so that had probably finished him off . . .

'I said, I'm not speaking to Memet,' said Constance, loudly. 'You're not listening.'

'Sorry,' said Scarlet, 'I was thinking.'

'What's he done?' asked Camille.

'Who knows?' said Constance. 'Who bloody knows?'

'Maybe he's run away with Barbs,' suggested Camille.

'Don't be silly,' said Scarlet to her daughter. 'Don't say such horrid things.'

'I'm not being horrid,' said Camille. 'You know what men are like.'

'I hope *you* don't,' said Constance, and Scarlet shuddered.

She lived in miserable anticipation of the day when Camille fell in love with some nightmare youth. The awful possibilities were endless. She supposed that if she were normal, she would be hoping for what was known as a 'nice boy' to come along, but she had no such faith. Some of the boys in the district were nice enough, but the nicest were too young for their years, while the others were alarmingly precocious. There seemed to be no happy mean.

'I wonder what happened to men,' she said as her second vodka sank lower in the glass. 'I mean they used to be taller. When I think about my mum, I always see her surrounded by tall men. She used to simper,' she added. 'She used to make them run round getting things for her – not my father; he used to make her get things for him – but a lot of them would run up and get her cardigan for her.'

'So they should,' said Constance.

'But they don't any more, do they?' said Scarlet. 'They don't wear tweed jackets and smoke pipes. Men have changed.'

'It's because they don't let them kill people any more,' said Constance. 'There aren't any soldiers. I mean, there *are*, but they're not real ones, not like they used to be. It's technology. They used to have to be brave, now they just have to hang around waiting for someone to press a button. No swords, no battle axes – just great big bangs and poison gas, so there's no call for bravery. They join the army on the off-chance nothing nasty's going to start, and then they make a shocking fuss when they're called on to do something.'

'I see,' said Scarlet, seeing that if there were no heroes, there was no one for anyone to emulate. There were only pop stars. 'How depressing,' she said.

'If there was a war,' said Camille, 'a real one, I mean – with Germany – Brian could wear a uniform and Mum could go and kiss him on the station platform and cry a bit.'

'You'd like that, wouldn't you?' said Scarlet starting on her third vodka: this was the dangerous one, the one that tended to make her either sad or irritable, depending on her mood before opening the bottle. If she had been cheerful, she would grow sad, and if she had been depressed, she would grow bad-tempered.

'You watch too many old films,' said Constance.

'I like war films,' said Camille. 'English ones with jolly brave chaps. American ones aren't any fun.'

'War is horrible,' said Scarlet.

'We know that, Mum,' said Camille. 'I didn't say I liked war. I said I liked war films – old English ones.'

'I prefer murder myself,' said Constance. 'Did I hear a knock?'

'I don't know. Did you?' asked Scarlet, staring into her glass.

Constance observed her. Scarlet should either stop drinking now or drink a lot more: she was never actually troublesome when she was intoxicated, but she could get argumentative and tedious. It was a pity: if she could only get good and fighting drunk, or even paralytic, it would ease a lot of her tensions.

'Someone *is* knocking,' said Camille.

'Go and see who it is, will you, there's a duck,' requested Constance, who had just made herself comfortable on the swinging seat. If it was Memet, she would prefer to greet him out here in the dusk, in darkness just burnished with the overspill glow from the street lamps, where he couldn't see her face.

'It's Tim,' said Camille, leading him into the garden.

'I thought you'd be here,' said Tim, 'when you weren't in at your place.'

'Perceptive of you,' said Scarlet.

Constance filled her glass. 'You sounded just like your mum then,' she said. 'Camille, get the boy a Coke from the fridge.'

'Can't we have a vodka?' asked Camille, seeing her mother wrapped in thought.

'No, you can't,' said Constance.

'We won't get drunk,' pleaded Camille.

'I don't give a toss whether you get drunk or not,' said Constance. 'You start on the vodka and there won't be enough for us.'

'Do you mind if we go over there?' asked Tim, indicating the end of the garden. 'I want to tell Camille something. It's not a secret, but I don't want to be in your way.'

'Help yourself,' said Constance. The lad had good manners, even if he was a cunning little sod – not a secret indeed!

'What's the matter?' inquired Camille under the hanging fronds of honeysuckle.

'Connie nearly caught me,' said Tim. 'I was casing Barbs's place and she came right into the garden. I had to dive in the corner and make like a garden gnome . . .'

'Why were you in Barbs's garden?' asked Camille.

'I told you – I was casing the joint,' said Tim.

'Oh, Sam got to you,' said Camille, enlightened. 'She wants to get her hands on the boy in the bistro.'

'She said she wanted to have a party,' said Tim.

'That's why,' said Camille. 'She wants to ask the boy from the bistro to it. I think it's very immature of her.'

'I could ask Chris,' said Tim.

'I wish you'd shut up about Chris,' said Camille.

'Anyway, I know how to get in,' said Tim. 'There's a ventilation thing in the kitchen window. You just have to push it through and put your arm in and unlock the catch.'

'And the next thing you know we're all in Holmes Road nick,' said Camille.

'What's wrong with you?' asked Tim. 'You in a bad mood or something?'

'No,' said Camille. The truth was that she didn't want Sam to be in love: not seriously in love with an older man, and the boy in the bistro wasn't really a boy at all, being at least twenty-two. Crushes were all very well, they'd all had crushes since they were seven, but Sam was nearly seventeen, and Camille could see her childhood slipping away. For as long as she could remember she had herself been in love with the man who led the greyhounds and their attendants on a dignified procession round the track before the race began. He wore riding-gear and a bowler, a stick tucked underneath his arm, and his air of unhurried authority gave him a matchless glamour. He held his shoulders well back and straight, and although Camille had never got close enough to make certain, she was convinced that he strode with his eyes half closed and a small, smart smile on his lips: unique, invincible, the splendid solitary leader of the procession, never to be challenged, usurped or tripped up. Ideal, glorious, imaginary man. When she was younger she had told Sam all about him whenever the occasion offered, but she couldn't do that now. Very soon Sam wouldn't be any fun any more. 'It's a silly idea,' she said, sulkily.

'What are those two whispering about?' asked Scarlet.

'Something or other,' said Constance.

'It's rude,' said Scarlet. 'Did I really sound like my mother?'

'Just for a moment,' said Constance, soothingly.

'My mother's awful,' said Scarlet. 'I think she's got a new boyfriend.'

'Strewth,' said Constance. 'How long's she mean to go on?'

'I don't know,' said Scarlet. 'But it's awfully undignified. Last time I rang her there was someone there. You could tell. She was putting on an act and laughing a lot.' The memory of her mother's trills rang in her ears.

'There was an old French lady carried on till they carried her out,' said Constance. 'Can't remember her name. Tim ought to know.' Scarlet couldn't see why Tim should know the name of some geriatric sex-pot and said so. 'No, she's famous,' said Constance. 'Though you're probably right. They don't seem to teach them anything these days.'

'Do you think my mother's *really* evil?' asked Scarlet.

'What?' said Constance.

'Evil,' said Scarlet, 'destructive. It's not very pleasant thinking your mother's bad all through.'

'You don't have to be a good woman to be a good mother,' said Constance. 'Rats make marvellous mothers – ask any rat. Film stars make terrible mothers, but that's because they don't know how to behave.'

'My mother isn't a good mother. She'd never have called me Scarlet if she was a good mother.'

'There's worse names,' said Constance.

'It isn't even a name, it's a description,' said Scarlet. 'They couldn't call me anything like *Mary* – oh, no – they had to be original, and I have to pay the price.'

'Cheer up,' said Constance. 'Cheer up. It's not so bad.'

'I'm a hopeless mother,' said Scarlet. 'It's all my mother's fault. She ruined her life and mine, and I've ruined mine and Camille's. Why did I call her Camille?'

'That's the drink talking,' said Constance. 'I bet you had no lunch.'

'There didn't seem any point,' said Scarlet. 'Everything's poisoned and I'm sick of thinking about it. The food's all poisoned, and the newspapers are poisoned, and television's poisoned, and Brian makes money telling people everything isn't – poisoned,' she concluded, sober enough to realize that she might not be expressing her thoughts with the clarity their profundity deserved. It seemed to her that she had had an insight of vivid and terrible power and that something should now change.

'You always say that when you're pissed,' said Constance. 'I'll make you a sandwich. You'll feel better when you've had something to eat.'

'I'd rather have another drink,' said Scarlet. 'Not a sandwich.' She closed her eyes.

'Mum drunk?' asked Camille, gazing down at her mother with apparently clinical detachment.

'Leave her there and let her sleep it off,' said Constance. 'What are you going to do?'

'Don't know,' said Camille. 'If Brian's not there, we might stay in.'

'If he *is* there,' said Constance, 'don't tell him she's here.'

'Of course not,' said Camille.

Alone in her garden with the sleeping Scarlet, Constance poured herself another drink. Something from the London sky fell into it. She removed it with her fingers, then she went and turned off the kitchen light and sat slowly swinging. If Memet came – but she knew he wouldn't come tonight. She counted as she swung – one, two, three – and wondered what he was doing. Whenever she told him she was never going to see him again he wept. That was one of the reasons she loved him, but she couldn't go on doing it indefinitely – swearing that this time he had gone too far and it was the end and then having to console him. Sometime she felt so fond of him that she inclined to a belief in reincarnation, feeling that they must once have been twins: she understood him far too well for her peace of mind, and she knew why her brothers detested him; apart from the fact that they were racists, they were baffled by his charm and his after-shave. They were old-fashioned and didn't believe in scent for men despite the efforts of people like Brian. It was annoying for them when their womenfolk smiled upon Memet, and it would have been inadvisable to hit him, since he came from a family as large as their own and as little troubled by the niceties of correct behaviour. When their wives strayed too far out of line they did indeed divorce them in the custom of the country but not before administering a thumping to all the parties concerned. Memet, however, was somewhat out of their experience, and they were wise enough to leave him alone. No matter what he got up to, Constance didn't want to see him damaged: it was the women she blamed, the tarts who ran after him. As far as she could remember, she hadn't thought like this about anyone before. She had regarded men as men had been used to regard women: pleasant and pleasurable enough when they stayed in line but outside the mainstream of life and more or less irrelevant to its principal purpose, which was keeping body and soul together with as little effort and as much comfort as was practically consistent with this aim. Her upbringing had not encouraged a romantic view of life. She had lived among and watched too many other lives. She made up her mind that if she found herself frequently lying sleepless and agitated, then Memet should, as far as she was concerned, be cast into outer darkness. Certainly no one should ever know just how much distress he could cause her.

'Where's your mother?' asked Brian.

'She went out,' said Camille.

'Where?' demanded Brian.

'She didn't say,' said Camille. Brian made himself a cheese sandwich and pushed the crumbs into a pile. 'That bread's gone mouldy,' Camille informed him.

Brian inspected his sandwich. 'No, it hasn't,' he said.

'Have it your own way,' said Camille.

'About art and commercialism,' said Brian, 'what you should say is this: that advertising has developed into a valuable art-form and the big international companies are the art patrons of today, but instead of just keeping one artist the industry employs thousands of talented people.'

'I'm not going to say that,' said Camille.

'Why not?' asked Brian.

'Because it's crap,' said Camille, simply.

'Actually, it isn't,' said Brian. 'If you think about it, you'll see that what I say is true. For the vast majority of people, who have no conception of good design, the images and logos of advertising are all they'll ever know of art. You could say, all they'll ever know of beauty. The familiar brand names with their images have taken the place of – statues and icons and the things people used to look at. Corporate design and familiarity are having an un-precedented, cohesive effect on society as well as bringing prosperity to the community.'

'What you mean,' said Camille, after a moment's thought, 'is, everyone drinks Coca-Cola and we'll have world peace.'

'That would be over-naive,' said Brian, 'but there is a broad sub-stratum of truth in it. Advertising is essentially democratic, knowing no bounds of class or colour and crossing all frontiers.'

'I was going to say art and commercialism were mutually exclusive,' said Camille grandly. She had asked Tim for his advice and thoughts on the matter, since Tim was undergoing a good education. 'Trollope hated advertising.'

'Trollope is hardly relevant to the present day,' said Brian, who had been educated differently.

'All right, I'll say what you said,' agreed Camille, who didn't care either way. 'It's a stupid project, however you look at it.'

'If you take my advice,' said Brian, 'and do what I tell you, you'll get top marks.'

'They probably won't bother to mark it,' said Camille. 'They just put a tick on it if you've done it at all. I gotta go now. Tim's upstairs.'

'What's he doing there?' asked Brian, who sometimes feared for Camille's virtue.

'He's helping me with my homework,' said Camille.

Tim was lying on her futon, smoking a Camel. 'Who're you talking to?' he inquired.

'It's Brian,' she said, 'but it's OK. He's in a good mood.'

'Ring Sam,' suggested Tim, 'and tell her to get her arse over here so I can tell her about the window.'

Camille dialled obediently. 'I still think it's a bad idea,' she said. 'You're going to drop yourselves in it.'

'You've got cowardly and craven in your old age,' said Tim, rolling over to stub out his cigarette in a crust.

Sam arrived in a state of excitement bordering on hysteria. 'He's coming,' she said. 'I asked him casually and he said he'd come.'

'Well, heavens to Betsy,' said Camille, coldly, using one of her grandmother's expressions. 'How perfectly marvellous.'

'Oh, he's *lovely*,' said Sam, smiling all over her face. 'He's gorgeous.'

'He's a waiter,' Camille reminded her.

'So's everyone,' said Sam. 'They just do it for money.'

'How disgusting,' said Camille, reflecting sadly on the way her friend was changing.

'I've got it all figured,' said Tim. 'I know how to get in.'

'And what if Barbs comes home in the middle of it?' asked Camille. 'What'll you say then?'

'Barbs wouldn't *care*,' said Sam, and Camille had to concede that Barbs was stunningly indulgent.

'All the same,' she said, for even Barbs might complain at finding her house taken over.

'Your mum's asked my mum to dinner on the sixth,' said Sam, 'so we'll do it then, when we know where they all are.'

'I think you're *mad*,' said Camille. They stared at her. 'You're very irresponsible,' she said.

'Who hasn't been to school this term?' asked Sam.

'I have been to school,' said Camille. 'I've been a lot.'

'And who dressed up as a wino and held up the off-licence?' asked Tim.

'I was only a child then,' said Camille, 'and it was only a joke.'

'Take no notice of her,' said Sam, 'she's just jealous.'

Camille was infuriated. 'People always say that,' she said, 'when they can't think of anything else to say. I'm the only sensible one here, and you're both being very child-ish.'

'Do shut up, Camille,' said Sam. 'You don't have to come if you don't want to. We can do it without you if you're going to be silly.'

'Ignore her,' said Tim pacifically. 'She'll change her mind. Let's think about the party. I'll ask Chris. We could have a barbecue.'

'Indoors?' asked Camille, who had again nearly lost her temper completely but retrieved it in the nick of time.

'What're you talking about?' asked Sam.

'I thought it was meant to be a secret,' said Camille. 'If you set fire to Barbs's back garden, people're going to notice.'

'No, we'll have it inside,' said Sam. 'We'll do it by candle-light.'

'They'll notice if you set fire to her house too,' said Camille.

'If you're going to be like that, I'm going home,' said Sam, but Camille had recovered her spirits.

'You could ask the fire brigade,' she said. 'Just in case. Firemen are sweet.'

'We'll tell everyone to bring a bottle, and if we get some money, we can telephone for pizzas so we don't have to do any cooking,' said Sam, her enthusiasm mounting again.

'Can we wear evening dress?' asked Tim.

'You can if you like,' said Sam, 'but that means we'll have to lay the table.'

'I'll do that,' said Tim, 'and I'll make the salad dressing.'

'*Camille,*' came a voice up the stairs.

'Oh, shit,' said Camille. 'Yeah?' she yelled.

'Do you know if your mother bought any butter today?' inquired Brian.

'If she did, it'll be in the fridge,' responded Camille at the top of her voice.

'It isn't,' said Brian.

'Then she didn't,' roared Camille. 'Honestly,' she said in her normal tones, lying back on the cushions.

'He's lonely,' said Tim. 'He can hear us laughing and he's all by himself down there.'

'Oh, what a terrible shame,' said Camille.

'We weren't laughing,' said Sam. 'We were talking.'

'When people are by themselves they always think other people are having a good time,' explained Tim.

'He hates to think of me having a good time,' said Camille. 'He'll be up in a minute. You wait.'

'Shall we go round to my place?' said Sam. 'Mum's on her own.' She was not in the least concerned at her mother's solitary state but knew her to be so recently buffeted by events that she would not cavil at two visiting teenagers, although she had intimated to Sam that if she filled the house with them, she would kill herself. 'They got no control, parents,' she added.

On their way downstairs they passed Brian, who was on his way up. 'Where are you going?' he inquired of Camille.

'Out,' she said, from the doorstep.

'When will you be back?' he cried, as she closed the door.

'Later,' she said. He couldn't hear her, but as that was what she always said, he assumed she'd said it again.

'You're awfully mean to him,' said Sam.

'You can talk,' said Camille. 'D'you ever hear yourself talking to Danny?' Danny was Sam's mum's ex-lover.

'That was different,' said Sam. 'Mum was going to marry him.'

'My mum did marry her one,' said Camille. 'That was

him asking me where I was going, in case you didn't notice.'

'Don't be clever,' said Sam. 'You know what I mean.'

'I don't know what they think will happen to us,' said Camille, 'with their example. You know any happily married people?'

'I don't think I know many *married* people,' said Sam, wrinkling her forehead, 'except the ones who're too ugly to find anyone else.'

'I know some,' said Tim, possibly out of contrariness.

'You're being Christian again,' said Camille. 'You're being stupid. People never used to get divorced like they do now.'

'It's the fault of advertising,' said Tim. 'You can put that in your project. Say everyone's encouraged to buy something new all the time.'

'It's not about marriage. It's about art,' said Camille.

'You can put it in as a footnote,' said Tim, 'and they'll think how intelligent you are.'

'Bollocks,' said Camille.

'D'you want to come and see how we can get in the window?' suggested Tim, as they passed Barbs's house.

'We'd better not,' said Sam. 'If they see us going in and out, they'll think we're up to something. Some crime-watcher'll ring the police and ruin everything.'

'I wonder where Barbs is?' said Tim, stopping and looking up at the bedroom windows.

'Oh, who cares?' said Camille. 'Let's go and get a video and some crisps.'

'I hope she's not dead,' said Tim. 'I don't like the idea of having a party in a dead person's house.'

'What're you frightened of?' asked Sam.

'I'm not frightened,' said Tim. 'I don't think it would be very nice, that's all.'

'He's being Christian again,' said Camille, and she and Sam giggled intermittently for the rest of the evening. Sam's mother endured it as patiently as she could. They'd grow out of it in time, she thought. And when Sam was old enough to leave home maybe she could lead a life of her own without prejudice.

Scarlet dreamed that an unknown person was kissing her and filling her mouth with ice-cold spit: she woke, glad that Constance, to whom she confided her dreams, was there to listen.

'How distasteful,' said Constance.

'I wonder what it means?' said Scarlet, who was feeling rather ill.

'It's a dream of death, I should think,' said Constance. 'Have a drink to take the taste away.'

'Where's Camille?' asked Scarlet.

'She went over to your place with Tim,' said Constance, reassuringly. 'Shall I make you a cup of something?'

'They said on the radio that toothpaste could make you ill. Crohn's Disease or something,' said Scarlet. 'Perhaps that's what I was dreaming about. A lot of skulls have very good teeth, when you come to think about it.'

'Now you're just being daft,' said Constance. 'Better have another vodka and cheer yourself up.'

'I don't think anything's going to cheer me up,' said Scarlet. 'Not as long as I'm alive. I don't *like* being alive,' she said. 'I don't believe I ever have, now I come to look at it.'

'So why're you always fussing about what they put in the fishpaste?' demanded Constance. 'The way you talk, you'd think you wanted to live for ever.'

'You're the same,' protested Scarlet. 'If anything, you make more fuss than I do.'

'But I do want to live for ever,' said Constance. 'There's the difference. It makes me mad to think Big Business is slowly polishing me off so's to increase its profit margins on pesticide.'

'I don't want to be old either,' said Scarlet. 'Just imagine how we'll feel if we get Alzheimer's.'

'We won't know much about it.' Constance was getting a little irritated with her friend. 'We'll just doddle about in a world of our own.'

'I already do,' said Scarlet. 'It must be awful being old and put away in a home because no one will have you at home and look after you.'

'Oh, do drop it,' said Constance. 'Your mother's not like that. She's got all her marbles and she looks after herself.'

'She doesn't know she's old,' said Scarlet. 'It hasn't dawned on her yet, and anyway she's always finding people to look after her, or so she thinks. Mostly they're ripping her off.'

'What you need's a holiday,' said Constance. 'I was feeling like jumping under a bus before I went away, then I felt better.'

'You haven't been sounding like a person who's feeling better,' said Scarlet. 'You've been bad-tempered.' She sat up.

'That's because of Memet,' said Constance.

'But you went away with Memet,' said Scarlet.

'And he came back before me,' said Constance. 'And d'you know what? The sun was just as hot, and the sea was just as wet, and the stars just as starry when he went away as when he was there. I was quite surprised. You know how you think the sun shines out of their backside, and when they're under your nose you don't have a minute's peace if they're not under your nose, if you see what I mean. Well, you don't mind half as much when they're miles away. If Memet went back to his village, I'd forget him in five minutes flat.' For a moment she closed her eyes and crossed her fingers. 'It's only when he's round the corner I mind him not being with me. Same with Barbs. If we knew she'd gone to climb the Himalayas, we wouldn't care. It's only that she might be passed out in the back yard.'

'It doesn't seem to matter now,' said Scarlet. 'I feel as though I'd been living under an anaesthetic for years and years.'

'What I'm saying is, what you need is a change,' said Constance. 'Maybe *you* should go and climb the Himalayas. You'd probably find you didn't care about anything except they put rancid butter in your tea . . . What d'you mean, anaesthetic?'

'Nothing seems real,' said Scarlet.

'Oh,' said Constance.

'The only feeling I seem able to feel is worry,' said Scarlet, 'and guilt. I used to worry about nuclear power, and now I worry about pollution and dead dolphins – when I'm not worrying about money. And the other morning I found myself feeling guilty about something I'd said to someone about twenty years ago. I don't think it's normal.'

'You *are* depressed,' said Constance, and Scarlet apologized.

'There doesn't seem to be anything to live for,' she said. 'I got off on the wrong foot, and I'm never going to get it right now. It's too late.'

'Nothing's ever too late,' said Constance, as people do in the face of this assertion, regardless of the truth. 'You should go and lie in the sun somewhere.'

'That gives you skin cancer,' said Scarlet.

'Oh, for God's sake,' said Constance, 'you could lie under a tree, couldn't you?'

But Scarlet was too far gone in disenchantment to look for a bright side. 'Once the novelty's worn off, everywhere's just like home,' she said, remembering the brief, pure joy of strange hotel rooms, which gradually became familiar as you unpacked the things you'd brought with you and acquired the kind of things you were wont to acquire, so that very soon you recognized yourself in your surroundings and understood that there was no escape. And yet she was aware of something lovely somewhere, something that was gone, or hidden, or yet to be attained: she supposed her therapist would say that this unrealistic shard of broken vision dated back to her infancy, when the human animal believes itself to be omnipotent, immortal and an integral part of all that is. Her therapist, she thought, was the most depressing person she knew, and that was saying something. She had defined what she perceived to be reality, and she kept trying to rub Scarlet's nose in it. Scarlet was beginning to believe she did it for reasons of her own, proselytizing for converts so as not to feel so lonely, so as to feel assured of the validity of her views, surrounded by like-minded people. Probably the reason why her therapist disapproved of her was not because she was – from a psychiatric standpoint – ill, but because she wouldn't get better.

'What're you thinking about now?' asked Constance.

'I was thinking Marx and Freud are the same,' said Scarlet, reflecting disparagingly on her therapist and on what she knew of the excesses of Josef Stalin for good measure. There was a bust of Marx in the local cemetery and a bust of Freud outside the swimming baths. It seemed odd when you came to consider it. 'I mean, they get these ideas and these bees in their bonnets and try and make everyone think the same way, and they change all the rules and upset everything, and Freud got it wrong in one way and Marx got it wrong in another.'

'Like the council,' said Constance, 'benefactors of human-ity and kidding themselves about the perfectibility of man – silly bastards.'

'That sort of thing,' agreed Scarlet.

'They got no grasp of reality,' said Constance.

'They think it's us who haven't,' said Scarlet.

'Yes, well, they're nuts,' said Constance.

'When my father died,' said Scarlet, 'his best friend was a philosopher, the sort that was in fashion then, and he kept telling me there was no after-life. I think he meant to be consoling. I think they think hope and faith are bad for you.'

'They think if you go round hoping and faithing, you won't do anything about conditions on the streets,' said Constance. 'Or maybe he thought your dad was bound for the other place.'

'I haven't got any hope and faith anyway,' said Scarlet, 'so he needn't have worried.'

'And you weren't all that fond of your dad, were you?' said Constance.

'No,' said Scarlet.

'Once upon a time I'd've made you turn religious,' said Constance, and suddenly it occurred to Scarlet that really she was already religious, as anyone who had borne a child must surely be: not in the conventional sense but rather as a passenger on a train would expect someone to be at the controls. The responsibility for bearing human beings was too great for a human being to bear: to bring a child into the world was a terrible thing to do unless you could be sure that there was someone at the end to take it out with at least as much love and care as you had brought it in with. The universe, thought Scarlet, must be benevolently staffed by more far-sighted beings than ourselves. There should be angels in the streets at check-points and at traffic crossings for we cannot be trusted . . .

'But the one true faith,' went on Constance balefully, 'have gone and fallen for that codswallop. Can you *believe* it? They prance about with their eyes closed, speaking in tongues. They've gone charismatic. You don't have to think if you're charismatic. You just sway around. You don't have to remember any words or facts or anything difficult like that – you just go off in a sort of coma and think how wonderful you are. It's very cold and horrible down here at the moment. I think God's sulking.'

'It does feel like that,' said Scarlet, wondering what she'd do without Constance, since there was no one else to talk to. 'Do you still believe in God?'

'I wouldn't know he was sulking if he wasn't there, would I?' said Constance. 'I mean, it's when they're sulking you *really* know they're there. He has turned away the glorious light of his countenance – or maybe the traffic fumes have got in the way, or maybe he's turned off the telly because of the charismatics.'

'Like Brian,' said Scarlet.

'I wouldn't compare Brian with God,' said Constance, 'but when he's sulking you don't half know it.'

'I know,' said Scarlet. 'I hate him.'

'Never mind,' said Constance. 'Maybe there'll be another one along in a minute.'

'I don't want another one,' said Scarlet, 'and I thought you didn't believe in divorce.'

'I don't believe in marriage,' said Constance, 'only you've

got to consider your hormones, and if you've got no skills, you've got to get married.'

'I haven't got any hormones,' said Scarlet. 'I can't remember what it was like when I did.'

'You need a holiday,' said Constance again.

'Maybe I should go where Barbs has gone,' said Scarlet.

'You think she's dead, don't you?' said Constance. 'You're going suicidal on me.' But Scarlet said she had to go home and see what was happening.

'Don't listen to me,' she said, 'I'll feel different tomorrow and we'll go out to lunch.'

'Oh, well,' said Constance, 'what's it matter?'

'That philosopher,' said Scarlet, who seemed to have forgotten about going home, 'the one I was telling you about, he used to go galloping after women all over the place when his hair and his teeth were all falling out, and he used to write about the terrific compassion he felt for the human race, and his breath was *foul*. My mother used to call him the Sage in bloom,' she added, 'when he was chasing women, that was.'

'Oh?' said Constance.

'It was a song,' explained Scarlet. 'All about deep in the heart of Texas and the sage in bloom being like perfume. Barbs isn't so old or so smelly, but she reminds me of him.'

'Very witty, your mother,' said Constance. 'She should write a book: *The Wit and Wisdom of Scarlet's Mum*.'

'She probably will,' said Scarlet. 'Most of her friends did. I can't think why she hasn't done it yet, now you come to mention it.'

'Might be interesting,' said Constance.

'Not to me it wouldn't,' said Scarlet. 'It would be embarrassing. I don't think I could bear it. It's dreadful being a daughter. I caught Cam looking at me the other day. I thought she'd got over being ashamed of me, but now she looks at me with contemptuous pity. It's very hard to take. I think I used to look at my mother like that.'

'You mean it's dreadful being a mother,' said Constance.

'I suppose I mean both,' said Scarlet.

'You aren't half confusing me,' said Constance. 'Any minute now you'll start moaning about being a woman.'

'No, I won't,' said Scarlet.

'I'd've laid odds you would,' said Constance, 'the way you were going on.'

'It's because I live here, I expect,' said Scarlet. 'You can't step into Sainsbury's without bumping into a lady in a boiler suit.'

'They've given up boiler suits,' said Constance, 'some time ago – except for the pregnant ones, and that's a mistake if you like.'

'I think I'm drunk now,' said Scarlet. 'I seem to be feeling awfully muddled.'

'You were going home half an hour ago,' said Constance.

'Consider me gone,' said Scarlet, but she didn't go. The rabbit, she thought tipsily, does not willingly gaze down the barrel of the gun. There was something wrong with this image and she struggled to clarify it. What she meant, she told herself, was that no living creature would choose to be a pet, and nothing would opt for imprisonment, and when she went home she'd feel trapped and, if she didn't know it was happening, she'd rather be shot – as long as she didn't see the bullet coming. 'Tell you what,' she said, 'I think Barbs has just run away.'

'What from?' asked Constance.

'Home,' said Scarlet. 'You know – all the responsibilities and all the things you have to do. Looking after people and not making a fuss when they do annoying things.'

'Barbs lived alone,' Constance reminded her. 'Except when she was doing grand larceny on someone else's husband.'

'She still had the four walls,' said Scarlet, 'and things to dust and wash up and hide from burglars. She still had to shake out the sofa cushions. I think she's taken to the open road like a Romany.'

'They don't do the open road any more,' Constance reminded her. 'They're living round the corner in the council yard.

'But *they*'re not real gipsies,' said Scarlet. 'They're tinkers.'

'True,' said Constance, who was herself beginning to feel slightly muddled. 'You know,' she said resentfully, 'when Billy was inside he was sharing a landing with some very funny men, and one day he was telling them about that pub he bought with the cellars full of Château d'Yquem – not showing off or nothing, just by way of general conversation, and they said, "Nice, is it, with that stuff you lot eat? Baked hedgehog and that?"'

'How uncalled-for,' said Scarlet.

'And when it was lights out they'd say, "Last one in pulls up the ladder."'

'What did they mean?' asked Scarlet.

'They were referring,' said Constance, 'to the old-style caravans with the steps up the back.'

'How rude,' said Scarlet.

'Just showing their ignorance,' said Constance. 'There wasn't a thing he could do at the time, but he's got his eye on them.'

Scarlet knew that Constance's family had firmly structured views on vengeance and a quick and subtle ear for a slight: sometimes they saw offence where none was intended, being – Scarlet allowed – not distinguished by great intelligence. It seemed that all the intelligence had gone to Constance, leaving her brothers with only wariness and guile to see them through the vicissitudes of life, although, Scarlet had to admit, they could be surprisingly kind. If she should mention to Constance that someone had treated her shabbily and Constance referred the matter to her brothers, they would uncomplainingly track down the brute and teach him manners. They were really, thought Scarlet, highly dangerous.

'Do you ever find yourself thinking opposite thoughts at the same time?' she asked.

'How d'you mean?' asked Constance.

'I'm not sure,' said Scarlet. 'I think I'm going mad.'

'Only sane people think that,' said Constance. 'Mad people think they're sane.'

'If I told my therapist that,' said Scarlet, 'do you think she'd let me go?'

'What d'you mean, let you go?' inquired Constance. 'She hasn't got you in thrall. She hasn't got you locked up in a room with a naked light bulb. She hasn't got control of your mind – at least I hope she hasn't. That wouldn't be good.'

'I feel I've got to explain something to her,' said Scarlet. 'I keep arguing with her in my mind, then when I see her I can't think of anything to say.'

'Say she's a silly, daft cow,' suggested Constance, who was rather jealous of Scarlet's therapist. 'Tell her to piss off.'

'I feel that would be irresponsible,' said Scarlet. 'Like kicking the St Bernard when he's only trying to help.'

'She's only trying to make a great deal of money,' said Constance. 'She's not plodding up and down the mountain-side with a barrel round her neck.'

'Anyway,' said Scarlet, 'we shouldn't be worrying about me. We should be worrying about Barbs. She might be lying dead in a ditch.'

'We've been through all that,' said Constance. 'Time and again we've been through all that. What you're doing is displacing your anxiety.'

'Am I?' said Scarlet.

'Yes,' said Constance, 'and you can tell your therapist I said so.'

'. . . So she's going to break into Barbs's house,' said Camille, 'and have her party there.'

'Oh, that's a good idea,' said Constance. 'That's really brilliant. You could put lipstick and some feathers on that one and take it for a walk.'

'I told her it was stupid,' said Camille, 'but she won't listen.' Constance was the only adult to whom she would dream of divulging Sam's plot, since whether Constance approved or not, she would not be difficult about it: clearly, she did not approve, either because the act would be an invasion of property and privacy or because it would land them all in trouble. Camille knew how earnestly Constance contrived to avoid trouble, having had enough, what with one thing and another, to last her a lifetime, as she often remarked. She was wont to say, she had done the white water and now she wished merely to paddle home. 'You tell her,' said Camille, none the less.

'I'm not getting involved,' said Constance, 'but you can tell her from me no good'll come of it.'

'It won't be the same if I tell her,' said Camille. 'She'd listen to you.'

'Well, she's not going to get the chance,' said Constance.

'I've got troubles of my own. Just don't you go getting mixed up in it, that's all.'

'I've got to,' said Camille, 'I'm her friend.'

'Then mind you stick near the door,' said Constance, 'and if anything starts, you get out quick.'

'She doesn't want that kind of party,' explained Camille. 'She wants the quiet kind.'

'Kids your age don't have the quiet kind,' said Constance. 'You know that.'

They turned into a muddy lane leading to the kennels. Mick's lay at the end of a row of long, low wooden buildings with a careful air: there were no guards or electric fences or anyone to be seen at all, but you got the feeling it would be inadvisable to appear shifty in any way as you traversed the path. Constance was aware of this. 'Mick,' she yelled, frankly, as they approached his door. It had his name painted above it.

As soon as she walked in Camille remembered the smell of dog. It mingled with the smell of dog's dinner which was simmering casually in a huge open vat: nameless portions of meat floated occasionally to the surface, nudging aside whole carrots. It was unappetizing.

'Lunch?' said Constance, gazing at the gently tossing surface.

'You want a coffee or something?' asked Mick, hospitably.

'Not at the moment, no,' said Constance. The smell was so all-pervasive that nothing consumed within half a mile of it could taste of anything not pertaining to dog.

'Camille?' said Mick, 'You want a coffee?'

'No, thank you,' said Camille. 'I'm all right.' It was not the smell which deterred her but the fact that there were two girls present: one sat on a table swinging her legs, while the other stood by a sink. She had the appearance of a person interrupted in what she was doing and regarded them unsmilingly. Camille felt intimidated and envious: she thought the girls didn't like the look of her and suspected she was after their jobs, and she felt like an interloper. The impression that everyone had been industrious until their arrival, and would be industrious when they had gone, grew stronger.

'So what've you been up to?' Constance asked of her brother.

'Just the usual,' said Mick. 'Had a couple of wins at the 'Stow. Not a lot.'

'Denise and the kids all right?' persisted Constance.

'They're OK,' responded Mick.

Camille wondered whether, if she was not here, he would be more expansive, then remembered that he had always been a man of few words.

'Want to have a walk round?' he invited.

'Yes,' said Constance, 'seeing as that's why we came. Camille wanted to see the dogs – relive her childhood.'

Again Camille felt awkward. She thought the girls would regard anyone who wanted to relive her childhood as wringingly wet, but they didn't openly sneer – just went back to whatever they'd been doing while Constance and Camille walked away to appreciate the fine lines and charming dispositions of twenty greyhounds.

Behind the kennels lay a paddock and beyond that a run, a path shadowed by shrubs and puny trees, the type of *rus in urbe* layout favoured by rapists.

'On the other hand,' amended Constance, who had just voiced this thought, 'it's the sort of place you might find nuns walking, telling their beads and saying their hours and stuff. Very secluded.'

'Not when the dogs are running,' said Mick. 'The sisters wouldn't like that.'

'I don't suppose the rapists would either,' said Constance.

'Why are the dogs so nice?' asked Camille. 'Why do they smile like that?' She would not have spoken thus in the presence of any of her own generation, but she was not being winsome: she was interested.

'It's the way their faces are made,' said Constance.

'It's not just that,' said Camille. 'The old one, the one with the bent leg, she definitely smiled at me. She did it last time, and she did it again.'

'Her name's Smiler,' said Mick. 'She does. We call her Mother.'

'See,' said Camille. 'I told you so.'

'I dare say,' said Constance, 'that I'd wear a smile on my face if all I had to do was lie around all day and every now and then chase a bit of fluff round a dog track. Not,' she added, 'that I'd be too keen on the food. I've never fancied boiled horsemeat somehow.'

'Some of that's best beef,' said Mick.

'You *do* spoil them,' said Constance. 'Still, a short life and a merry one, as they say.'

Camille considered this thoughtless of Constance. Most of the dogs were put down when they slowed up, but it seemed indelicate to refer to it.

'It's a cruel, cruel world,' said Constance. 'You bring them on from the time they're little, and they think they've got it made, then – wallop.'

'Here's Mother,' said Mick, placidly, as though to deny her assertion. Mother, naturally, had not raced since she broke her leg some years before, but she went round without let or hindrance like an eldest wife or mother-in-law from some older, more civilized society, self-possessed, amiable and grave, all passion spent.

'She caught a pigeon the other day,' said Mick, as they passed a pile of feathers.

'So what do you think?' asked Constance of Camille.

'I think it's lovely,' said Camille, wiping away a tear as she thought of the joyful, urgent creatures, little more than puppies, having to be put to death. She hoped that Constance would not embarrass her by telling Mick that she wished to be a kennel-maid: she'd changed her mind anyway.

'I must say,' said Constance, 'it's nice to see a lot of animals sitting peacefully in their kennels like a lot of monks. When you see those wildlife programmes on telly they're all either fucking or eating each other. It puts you off your tea.'

'That's typical of the media,' said Camille. 'They always show the most violent aspects of everything so's to make money.'

'She's got it in for her stepfather,' Constance explained to Mick. 'He's in advertising.'

'He's not so bad,' said Camille, feeling suddenly alien and rather lost in these surroundings. When she was younger and thoroughly impatient with her mother she had sometimes entertained a fantasy that Constance would kidnap her and take her away to live with the gipsies: now she felt that she might not have liked it as much as she thought. It would take her a long while to learn to become one of them. For the first time she really wondered where Barbs was, whether she was frightened somewhere, cold and alone. Her eyes filled with tears again, not only for pity at the death of dogs.

'They don't feel a thing,' said Constance. 'Honest. Do they, Mick?'

'Not a thing,' said Mick.

'Me and Memet'll take you racing soon,' promised Constance, and Mick said nothing. Then again, thought Constance, maybe it was time now for Memet to leave the stage. He hadn't been round for days. Maybe he'd left the stage of his own accord. Perhaps she should put her money where her mouth was and forget all about him: if she concentrated hard enough, she could work herself up to not caring about him – perhaps.

'You're a cliché' Scarlet remarked to her reflection in the dressing-table mirror. 'You're a living, breathing, walking, talking cliché. And, what's more, you talk to yourself. If the part wasn't already over-subscribed, you could be the Mad Woman of the district. You could go round with a lampshade on your head, or join the loonies in the Buddhist robes, or sit outside the Drop-in Centre all day with a can of Special Brew in your hand. Or perhaps you don't need to. Perhaps it's enough to be Scarlet, who has to see a therapist and dreams only of early retirement and death. Perhaps you could change your name to Gamboge Yellow and be a different person. Perhaps you could go and fight in one of those wars they're always having somewhere and lose yourself in the din of battle. Perhaps,' she said in the words of Constance, 'you could just shut up, you silly, daft cow.'

Brian, emerging from the bathroom, heard his wife talking and imagined she was with Camille, thus he was surprised to find her alone.

'Where's Camille?' he asked.

'She's gone to Sam's party,' said Scarlet, hastily, applying the brush to her hair and wondering why it made you feel so odd if you looked at yourself for a long while in the glass.

'Who were you talking to then?' said Brian.

'Nobody,' said Scarlet, thinking that if you looked at yourself for long enough, you and your reflection merged until there really was no one there at all. You were cancelled out. No one at all.

Brian opened his mouth to tell his wife she was a liar and then realized that that would be too strong. He was afraid she was going off her head, and this made him unreasonably irritable. When your family members went mad these days you had to keep them at home, and whatever the sound policies, on the part of the government, which lay behind this decision, it was undoubtedly inconvenient for those upon whom would fall the burden of caring for the deranged. Then he saw the look of misery on her face and was seized by fear. A sad, mad person was more than anyone could be expected to bear. It would be appalling to have a crazy wife, but if you also felt sorry for her, how could you be expected to cope?

'Darling,' he said, 'what *is* wrong?' He spoke so gently that Scarlet half rose from her stool: it was bad enough going mad without causing your husband to pity you. Compassion could only lead to increased confusion, for it would be wasted on her. She had no idea of how she might use it: draining him of pity would be worse than draining him of money, and she would drown in guilt. Besides, he'd never be able to sustain it for more than a minute or two.

'Nothing's wrong,' she said. 'I'm just a bit tired.'

He wanted to ask what *she* had to be tired about, to remind her that this dinner-party was all her idea, and there was no real point to it at all, since they had asked nobody whom they needed to impress. 'We'll try and get rid of them early,' he said. 'You must get a good sleep.'

Downstairs Scarlet put what are known as the 'last

touches' to her dinner table, reflecting that this was a term an undertaker might employ in the course of his duties. There were even flowers and candles, and the table was shrouded in white. 'Oh, for God's sake, Scarlet,' she said.

'Can I do anything, darling?' asked Brian.

'You could make sure I've put enough glasses in the drawing-room,' said Scarlet. 'And check on the whisky.'

'Do you want a drink?' suggested Brian, still on that cherishing note which so disconcerted his wife.

'Not yet,' said Scarlet, who had already slugged back a double.

'Well, I think I'll have one,' said Brian, and Scarlet saw that things were even worse than they seemed, for now his tone was artificial: he was making conversation about something so trivial as pouring himself a drink.

'Did you have a good day at the office?' she asked, hearing herself with horror.

Even Brian thought this was going too far: he paused at the door and turned, looking at her, puzzled.

'Not bad,' he said.

Scarlet wondered if he thought she was trying to catch him out. 'Make sure Nigel doesn't eat the crisps,' she said. 'He likes crisps.'

'Bloody cat,' said Brian, more normally.

'Bloody knives and forks,' said Scarlet under her breath, 'bloody mats and napkins. Bloody chicken pie.'

'Enjoying yourself?' asked Constance, appearing from the back garden.

'You smell wonderful,' said Scarlet.

'Came by some scent,' said Constance vaguely. 'Good stuff. None of your Californian Poppy. I'll let you have a bottle.'

'Will you count the mats for me?' asked Scarlet, 'And

then the people. I always get it wrong. I always include someone else – someone I can't remember.'

'Who's coming?' inquired Constance. 'Anybody gorgeous?'

'Brian, Connie, Scarlet, Pam, Clarissa and Guy – I make that six,' said Scarlet, counting on her fingers with her eyes closed.

'So do I,' said Constance. 'What a coincidence.'

'There are too many women,' said Scarlet.

'There always are,' said Constance.

'Should I've asked Memet?' asked Scarlet.

'I doubt if you could've found him,' said Constance. 'He seems to have done a runner. He's disappeared.'

'Everyone keeps disappearing,' said Scarlet and then wished she hadn't. Constance said nothing but walked back into the kitchen, where she lifted the lid off the soup and stood staring at it.

'Green pea,' said Scarlet. 'I used dried ones and I'm going to put some frozen ones in at the last minute.'

'It's a very pretty colour,' said Constance, 'and full of something or other.'

'I don't care what it's full of,' said Scarlet. 'I wouldn't care if it was full of cat's pee.'

'Dear, dear,' said Constance, 'You're in a rare good humour. You're sorry now you asked those people, aren't you?'

'Of course I am,' said Scarlet, 'I always am, but I never learn. Have a drink. I got two bottles of Scotch and I hid one down by the dishwasher.'

'That's an alcoholic's trick,' said Constance, interestedly. 'Only if you really were an alcoholic, you wouldn't've told me.'

'I expect I would,' said Scarlet. 'I tell you everything.' The door bell rang. 'Oh, shit,' she said.

'You never used to swear,' said Constance. 'Not until you met me,' she added complacently, as Scarlet went to the door.

Brian was there before her, saying, 'Come in.' She wished he wouldn't: once the door was opened, of course they were going to come in. What did he think?

Out of an old, half-moribund loyalty she repeated his words. 'Do come in.'

'You know everyone,' said Brian, indicating Constance, who had beaten them to it into the drawing-room.

'Hello, Constance,' said Clarissa. 'I've been meaning to ask if you'd seen anything of Barbs.' She and Guy lived over the road, next door but one to Barbs's house.

'Funny you should say that,' said Constance. 'Hi, Guy.'

'Clarissa's a bit worried,' said Guy, as though worrying was woman's work.

'I'm not worrying exactly,' said Clarissa, as though worrying was shameful, 'only she went without saying anything, and it's not like her.'

'That's true,' said Constance.

'I keep wondering,' said Clarissa, 'whether that woman who was pulled out of the canal could be anything to do with Barbs. It says in the paper they haven't identified her yet.'

'D'you mean you think it's her?' asked Constance, irritated at this roundabout way of expression. 'Did she fall or was she pushed?'

'It did cross my mind,' said Clarissa. 'It did say in the paper she was between thirty and forty, well nourished and well dressed.'

'Then it can't've been Barbs, can it?' said Constance, chewing crisps, vulgarly, with her mouth open. 'She goes round looking like something the cat dragged in.' She didn't like Clarissa, and Clarissa, for her part, was not very fond of Constance.

'Her things were all good-quality,' said Clarissa stiffly, turning to talk to someone more civilized.

Camille, who had sneaked in unseen to borrow the garlic-crusher, overheard this exchange and smiled. She couldn't stand Clarissa who, in the past, had quite often perceived it as her duty to inform Scarlet that her daughter, in one way or another, had been up to no good. The door bell rang again and Camille hid in the downstairs lavatory until she could make her getaway. When she heard the voice of Sam's mother she realized for the first time that it was more than likely that her own mother would, during the course of the evening, make some reference to the dinner-party which, she had been led to believe, was taking place in Pam's house. Camille accused herself of lack of foresight and rapidly made up a yarn whereby they had thought better of the dinner-party and had spent the evening playing Monopoly at Tim's place in a blameless fashion. In the meantime her mother would worry, but there was nothing she could do about that at the moment.

'Drink, Pam?' asked Brian. Well, of course she wants a drink, thought Scarlet, what does he think she came for?

'Just a small one,' said Pam, 'if that's whisky. And a lot of water.'

'Don't want to drown it,' said Brian.

Scarlet made a sudden movement.

'We were just talking about Barbs,' said Clarissa. 'You haven't seen her recently, have you?'

'The last time I saw Barbs,' said Pam acidly, 'she was massaging Danny to relieve his tension.'

'Where?' asked Clarissa. 'I mean, where was she? Not where she was massaging him.'

'In my sitting-room,' said Pam, 'and she was massaging the back of his neck, if anyone's interested. It was weeks ago, just before I threw him out.'

'Typical,' said Constance. 'Couldn't keep her hands off anything in trousers.'

'That's not fair,' said Clarissa. 'She's kind-hearted . . .'

'She likes to be liked,' explained Constance.

'We all do,' interrupted Clarissa.

'. . . only while she's getting herself liked by one load of people, she's getting herself disliked by another load,' continued Constance. 'She's a troublemaker. Soon as she sees something going wrong, she comes bowling round spreading sweetness and light, and that just makes it worse.'

'She was very kind to me when the children had mumps,' said Clarissa. Constance gave her up.

'Clarissa was wondering if we should go to the police,' said Guy.

'We wondered that too,' said Scarlet, 'but it seems so dramatic. She hasn't been gone long after all. She could be anywhere. Now I come to think of it, I don't know much about her family at all – only that she's got a sister and a mother somewhere in the States.'

'Oregon,' said Guy. Constance looked up from her glass and gazed at him.

'You obviously knew her better than I do,' said Scarlet, growing confused with her tenses, for she had begun to identify Barbs with the sodden creature they had lifted from the canal.

'I hardly knew her at all,' said Guy, unconcernedly, 'only she happened to mention it once.' Constance was still gazing at him, swinging her foot gently and clasping her glass with both hands.

'Not a very cheerful conversation,' remarked Brian.

'I must go and look at the chicken pie,' said Scarlet.

Brian said, 'Would you like me to do it?', astonishing his wife.

'You wouldn't understand what it means,' she said. 'You have to assess its colour and everything. Connie, you can come and help.'

'Smells all right,' said Constance, neutrally.

Scarlet turned the oven down. 'I cannot think what's come over Brian,' she said. 'Imagine him volunteering to look at the chicken pie. He must've gone crazy.'

'It's funny,' agreed Constance..

'I've just got to make the dressing,' said Scarlet. 'Where the hell's the garlic-crusher?' She flung the salad together pell-mell with no hint of arrangement. Clarissa did things differently. She served restaurant meals, laying the table with dire artistry, wrapping mousses of fish in fillets of different fish, lapped by puddles of brightly hued sauces, and she provided each guest with his own little plateful of miniature carrots, mange-tout peas and tiny potatoes. She moulded rice and puréed sprouts, slid paper garters on to lamb bones and rolled slices of beaten meat around stuffings which, as often as not, contained pine kernels. Scarlet despised her methods, as she knew Clarissa would despise hers, for Scarlet agitated herself only about the nutritional content of food and held in contempt the misplaced aestheticism of the lily-contoured table napkin.

They were talking about advertising when Constance and Scarlet went back upstairs. Scarlet addressed herself to Pam. 'I hope they're not making too much mess,' she said.

'Sorry?' said Pam.

'The kids,' said Scarlet. 'The dinner-party. I hope they're not ruining your kitchen.'

'Do you mind if I use the phone?' requested Pam. 'There's

no answer,' she said after a while. 'Are you sure it was tonight?'

'I think so,' said Scarlet.

'At my place?' asked Pam.

'That's what they told me,' said Scarlet.

'I'm not going to worry about it now,' said Pam, resolutely, 'but if they leave it like last time, I'll kill them.'

'I am sorry,' said Scarlet. 'I felt sure you knew.'

'Knew what?' asked Clarissa, turning to them.

'Oh, it's nothing,' said Pam. 'The girls are up to something, that's all. I expect it's all right.' She, too, had suffered from Clarissa's neighbourly concern about the behaviour of her child and was waiting with calm anticipation for the time when Clarissa's children, who were at present eleven and twelve, should enter puberty. 'How are your two?' she inquired.

'They're fine,' said Clarissa. 'We're wondering if we should send Siân to La Sainte Union.'

'You can't,' said Constance. 'You've got to be Catholic.'

'Are you sure?' asked Clarissa.

'I should be,' said Constance. 'I spent all my formative years there.'

'She got eight O levels and three A's,' said Scarlet.

'But on the whole I'm an autodidact,' said Constance, fairly confident that Clarissa wouldn't have a clue what she meant by this.

'We heard it was a good school,' said Clarissa, acidly.

'I should think everything's ready now,' said Scarlet. 'Shall we go down?'

'An opsimath,' added Constance dreamily, descending the stairs.

'I'm *telling* you,' said Sam, 'I'm telling you, she's gotta be dead because no one, but *no one*, would go away without her make-up.'

'What were you doing in her bedroom?' asked Tim.

'It was in the bathroom, clever,' said Sam. 'But now you mention it, I'm going to go and look in her bedroom too. If her drawers are full of clean nighties and stuff, then she's definitely dead.'

'You can draw no real conclusions from any of that,' said Tim. 'She might've had two lots of make-up, and you don't know how many nighties she's got.'

'You're just a spoil-sport,' said Sam. 'You got no sense of adventure.'

'It was I who broke in,' Tim reminded her. 'I think that was very brave and daring, considering my conscience and my reputation as a law-abiding person.'

'And people don't have two lots of make-up,' said Sam. 'She's left all her moisturizers and her rejuvenating creams and her eye-liner and everything. She might have her lip-gloss in her handbag, but she wouldn't go off without her Estée Lauder. And you only broke in to show how smart you are, not because you're so brave.' Sam was thoroughly disgruntled because the boy from the bistro had failed to appear. She had waited behind the hedge in the front garden, ready to smuggle him into the house without alerting the neighbours, but he never arrived: she had drunk half a bottle of white wine as she waited and now felt slightly sick.

Camille was being elaborately tactful. 'I expect they were very busy at the bistro,' she said.

'Oh, shut up,' said Sam.

'No, really,' said Camille, suppressing a gratified smile. She made an effort to feel some true sympathy, but it was difficult – she supposed that she wouldn't be able to experience compassion in a deep and real sense until she'd had some children, since only matters like the putting down of young greyhounds brought tears to her eyes. Growing up was much harder than was ever said, involving, as it must, both the practised, clinical coldness to which she aspired combined with a proper sense of pity when it was called for and could be expressed with dignity and without embarrassment to the parties concerned. She was torn between the urge to dance around saying 'Nah, nah – he didn't come,' and an inclination to draw Sam's head upon her shoulder and stroke her hair soothingly: it was impossible to know which would have maddened Sam more. 'Anyway, I'm starving,' she said.

'It isn't ready,' snapped Sam.

Camille knew that it could have been but understood that Sam was putting dinner off until the last possible moment in case the boy from the bistro turned up, breathless and apologetic, because his motorbike had broken down and he'd had to walk.

'So, what'll we do?' she demanded. 'We can't play music, and there's nothing on telly, and it'll be dark soon. I think Sam's right. We might as well explore and look for clues. It could be our duty, seeing as we're in here anyway.'

'There's one already,' said Sam, pointing at the windowsill.

'Where?' asked Camille.

'That's Memet's hat,' said Sam.

'How d'you know?' asked Camille, who was protective towards Constance and reluctant to believe that her beloved Memet could be untrue.

'You know anyone else who'd wear a hat like that?' asked Sam.

'So he probably came to tea and forgot it,' said Camille.

'I'm going to look for real clues round here – bloodstains and things.'

'And you can come with me,' said Sam to Tim, 'and I'll show you her make-up bag.'

'I don't suppose I'll deduce much from it,' said Tim.

'You just gotta *see* it,' said Sam stubbornly, 'and then you'll believe me.'

'I do believe you,' said Tim, 'only I can't see it matters.'

'That's because you're just stupid,' said Sam. 'Any woman would see *immediately*.' She was accustomed to the barriers to understanding between the sexes, but it never ceased to annoy her: it was one of the reasons she had had to expel her mother's lover. 'We'll look in here first,' she said. The front bedroom was almost sure to be Barbs's, since most people in the district chose the front bedroom for themselves, even though it was quieter at the back. The bed was roughly made, the duvet pulled up, but there were clothes lying on it. 'See?' said Sam.

'See what?' asked Tim.

'You don't leave your bedroom like this if you're going away. You leave it tidy for when you come back.'

'*You* don't,' said Tim.

'I've got Mum,' said Sam. 'When *she* goes away she leaves it tidy.'

'The kitchen was quite tidy,' said Tim. There weren't any plates of half-eaten meals or cups of cold coffee.

'You always leave the kitchen tidy,' explained Sam, 'in case somebody calls. You needn't bother so much with your bedroom because you can do it later.'

'I think you're making a fuss about nothing,' said Tim. 'It all looks perfectly normal to me.'

'It would look normal to you,' said Sam, 'if a herd of wild animals had run through it. You don't understand women.'

'I don't want to,' said Tim, rather huffily; Sam's virtuous and superior tone was beginning to irritate him.

'Sam,' called Camille, and her voice sounded strange.

'Yes,' cried Sam, eagerly – for the boy from the bistro might have silently arrived.

'Come here,' said Camille.

'Whatsa matter?' said Sam, sliding downstairs.

'Look,' said Camille, holding up a Chanel-type handbag with a brass chain, 'you just might forget your make-up, but you wouldn't forget this.' She opened it wide to let them see the contents.

'What'll we do?' asked Tim after a short silence; even he had to admit that a lady would not go away leaving behind all her credit cards and a wad of paper money.

'Where was it?' asked Sam.

'Down beside the sofa in the sitting-room,' said Camille. 'All by itself.'

'We'd better tell someone at once,' said Tim. 'We could say we were passing and we saw something suspicious, so – no, that won't do.'

'It won't really, will it?' said Camille. 'Seeing as there's a pan of spaghetti boiling on the stove and a green salad sitting in the sink and an enormous gâteau on the table and flowers and napkins and everything.' This reminded Sam of the dereliction on the part of the boy in the bistro, and she bit her lip. 'We can't really say we saw something suspicious, so we climbed in the back window, and then we just thought we'd have a dinner-party while we were here. That doesn't sound too kosher somehow. It lacks something . . .'

'Sarcasm doesn't suit you,' said Tim.

'So, what *are* we going to do?' asked Camille.

'You'll have to let me think,' said Tim. 'I wonder if

Chris is coming. He had a lot of prep, but he said he'd try. He'd have some idea.'

'I knew we'd get into trouble,' said Camille.

'We haven't got into trouble,' said Sam, 'not yet, and why don't you just shut up?'

There was a knock at the front door.

'*Shit!*' said Camille. They stood looking at the door, wondering what form the knocking threat would take. It was some moments before it occurred to any of them that it might well be Chris or the tardy boy from the bistro, harmlessly appealing for admission to his promised evening of jollity and sustenance.

'What if it's Barbs?' whispered Camille. 'Or the police?'

'Come back for her handbag, I suppose,' said Sam. 'She's just noticed she's not had it for a week or so.'

'Ssshh,' said Camille.

'I'm going to open the door,' said Sam, striding forward, since her hope that it would be the boy from the bistro was greater than her fear of retribution.

'Am I awfully late?' he said.

'Oh, God,' said Camille. 'I think I've wet myself.' Sam gave her a look of furious disapproval, worse than that of any mother, for love was here at stake. Camille put her tongue out at her friend's back as she ushered her guest downstairs. 'We'll get no sense out of her now,' she said to Tim. 'What'll we do?'

'It'll give me time to think,' said Tim. 'I'll think of something.'

'It's going to be a wonderful evening,' said Camille, 'with her drooling over the waiter, and me nearly dying of fright at the slightest sound, and you sitting there thinking.'

'What are you two whispering about?' called Sam, sounding mature. 'Come on downstairs and join us.'

When Camille entered the open-plan area that was Barbs's kitchen and dining-room, she realized she was still holding Barbs's handbag, and she put it on the table with a swift, rejecting movement as though it was hot or unclean. Sam smoothly removed it to the window-sill.

'Nothing's so much fun as it used to be,' said Camille, for no apparent reason.

'Have a drink,' said Sam. 'Tim, will you drain the spaghetti?'

'We haven't made the sauce yet,' said Tim.

'So, put the spaghetti in the oven to keep warm,' suggested Sam, endeavouring to do as little as possible by bossing people about and yet maintaining an irresistible charm of manner: she wanted to sit by the boy from the bistro while someone else did what work remained to be done. 'The sauce won't take long,' she said. They were making it from a tin of clams, a tin of sweetcorn, garlic and a carton of double cream. Sam had had something similar in Italy, although she had never worked out what the precise ingredients were. 'You haven't really met Joe, have you?' she said to Camille.

'Hello,' said Camille, smiling falsely.

'Nice house,' said Joe, sitting down, for he was still young enough to make himself instantly at home.

'It's a friend's house, really,' said Sam, rather wishing to tell him that her own house was even nicer.

'She's disappeared,' said Camille, loudly.

'Why don't you make the salad?' inquired Sam in her dangerous voice, but Joe seemed unperturbed.

'Really?' he said.

'Vanished without trace,' said Tim, asserting himself. He would not, himself, have mentioned the matter, but now it was out in the open it would provide something to talk about. Without loud music these small gatherings of very young people could make hard going. 'Nobody's seen her for a week, and she's not taken any of her stuff.'

'I told you that,' said Sam, indignantly, 'and you told me not to be so stupid.'

'That was before we found her handbag,' said Tim.

'*I* found it,' said Camille.

'Perhaps aliens have taken her,' suggested Joe, not giving the impression that it concerned him very greatly. Sam hoped he wasn't one of those New Age mystical types. The bistro was situated close to the occult bookshop. She and Camille, possibly under the influence of the Westminster boys, were scornful of most aspects of the various flourishing cults, although they read their horoscopes avidly.

'There aren't any aliens,' said Camille. 'Connie says it's easier to hide bodies than you might think. You bury them under bits of the motorway, and if the motorway's finished, you put them on a traffic island with bushes on it. No one ever walks round a traffic island. And if you want to find out if you're being followed, you have to drive round traffic islands twice, and then, if another motor does it too, you know it's following you.'

'What does Connie know about it?' asked Sam crossly. She too liked Connie, but she wasn't as close to her as Camille was.

'Connie knows a lot of villains,' said Camille, as one who once might have said, 'She knows a lot of dukes.' She opened the tin of clams.

'She says so,' said Sam, obeying the universal compulsion to quell a name-dropper, 'but she exaggerates.'

'You don't know her,' said Camille, in the usual way of name-droppers. 'You don't know her like I do.' She opened the tin of sweetcorn and stirred it into a pan with the clams and the cream.

'You're supposed to heat them up first,' said Sam, 'and add the cream at the last minute.'

'*You* do it then,' said Camille.

'It's too late now,' said Sam and, just in time, remembered her role of imperturbable hostess and *femme fatale*. 'I expect it'll be all right,' she said, gracefully.

'It stinks,' said Camille, sniffing.

'It's only the garlic,' said Sam, with a light laugh.

'I haven't put the garlic in yet,' said Camille. 'I think the clams are off. I told you we should have ordered a pizza.'

'Here, I'll do it,' said Tim. 'Where's the garlic-crusher?' He had a pacific nature.

'Why do you say there aren't any aliens?' asked Joe, who had been sitting apparently lost in thought.

'Because there aren't,' said Camille. 'You ever seen one?'

'Have you ever not seen one?' inquired Joe.

'Yes, all the time,' said Camille. 'Every day I don't see one.'

'You don't know that,' said Joe.

'Yes, I do,' said Camille.

Sam began to despair of her evening. Abandoning caution, she got up and turned on Barbs's tape machine. Instead of the expected music there came the sound of voices. Sam listened.

'You're thinking of little green men,' continued Joe. 'You don't know what aliens look like. I could be an alien. For all I know,' he conceded generously, 'you could be one.'

If she hadn't been so irritable and on edge, Camille might have been flattered by this notion. As it was, she rejected it out of hand. 'Nuts,' she said.

'Sshh. Listen,' said Sam. Barbs's voice, soft and seductive, drifted from the machine.

'Blimey,' said Tim after a moment.

'Sshh,' said Sam. There was a man's voice now and other sounds.

'Well, that's it,' said Camille, after a further moment. 'You wouldn't go away and leave that for anyone to hear. Not unless you were out of your mind.' Her voice was unsteady. 'Isn't it funny,' she said, 'how you can't *like* people when they're doing that.'

'Sshh,' said Sam again, flapping her hand imperatively. 'I know that voice.'

They listened.

'It could be anybody, going "Ooh" and "Ah",' said Camille. 'Stupid prat.'

'Shut up,' said Sam. 'Damn, now I've missed it. Put it back to the beginning.'

'No way,' said Camille. 'It's rude.'

'I think this is ready,' said Tim, from the stove.

'I've been put off my dinner,' said Camille.

'Don't be childish,' said Sam, but she turned off the tape.

'I will if I like,' said Camille. 'If I like, I'll throw my dinner on the floor and put clams in my hair and have tantrums, and . . .'

'You were always doing that when you were little,' said Sam. 'I'd've thought you'd've grown out of it by now.'

'If we don't eat soon,' said Tim, 'this ineffably delicious dish will either burn to a crisp or go cold, depending on how I decide to proceed. I can leave it on the stove or take if off, and either way it won't be the same as it would be if we ate it now.'

'Well, just put it out and stop fussing,' said Sam. 'I don't know what you're going on about.'

'Oh, sorry,' said Tim. 'I just got the impression you were going to go on arguing all night.'

'I never argue,' said Sam.

'Yes, you do,' said Camille.

'No, I . . .'

'I'm putting it out now,' said Tim. 'After we've eaten we can go round to the pub and play snooker. Chris might be there.'

'I'm sick of the sound of Chris,' said Camille.

'You wait till you've met him,' said Tim.

'He's very good-looking,' said Sam.

'Chris what?' asked Joe. 'There's a Chris comes into the bistro a lot.'

'Probably the same one,' said Tim. 'He's always around.'

'I don't care,' said Camille. 'I don't care if he looks like Rudolph Valentino and goes in every bistro in the country every night of the year. I'm not interested in men.'

'She's a late developer in some ways,' said Sam.

'Who's Valentino?' asked Joe.

'He was a friend of my grandmother's,' said Camille. 'I think. She always said he was good-looking. My grandmother's mad about men,' she added. 'And a fat lot of good it's done her.'

'She enjoys herself,' said Sam.

'Yeah, but she's a bit disgusting,' said Camille. 'You've got to admit that.'

'A bit,' conceded Sam, 'but she doesn't let things get her down . . .' Here she emitted a shriek of laughter before continuing, and the others looked at her inquiringly. 'Get her down,' said Sam. 'Oh, never mind. What I mean is she enjoys life.'

'She's sixty if she's a day,' said Camille, who found it difficult, in her more regressive moments, to believe that anyone over the age of about twenty could find much reason for living.

'Some people are like that,' said Sam, obscurely. 'Film stars and stuff.'

'It's still a bit disgusting,' said Camille, who had followed her friend's train of thought.

'I used to think that when I was younger,' said Sam. 'I thought Mum was much too old to carry on like that.'

'Was that why you told Danny she shaved?' asked Camille, who had been present on that occasion.

'That was one of the reasons,' admitted Sam. 'I was very childish then, but I wanted him to go away. He was a complete arsehole.'

'She wasn't half mad with you,' said Camille.

'I was sorry for her, afterwards,' said Sam. 'It was really mean of me.'

'Girls can be really nasty,' said Tim.

'You can just shut up,' said Camille, leaping to her friend's defence, for she would not permit a male to speak ill of her. 'What do you know about it? Men can be pretty nasty too. You should hear Brian when something gets up his nose.'

'But we're more honourable,' said Tim, unwisely. 'We look after you.'

'Do me a favour,' said Camille, wearily, suddenly mature, but Sam screamed with rage, remembering Danny and his idleness and greed. She regretted it almost immediately, for the boys looked embarrassed, not ashamed of themselves, as they should have been, but shy in the face of a tasteless demonstration.

'Let's go down the pub,' she suggested, as her temper ebbed.

'What about the salad?' asked Tim.

'And the gâteau?' said Camille.

'We can have them later,' said Sam, recklessly, swallowing a mouthful of strange-tasting spaghetti. 'We can go down the pub and come back and eat them then.' The truth was that she was disappointed in the boy from the bistro. He looked less glamorous without his uniform of short white apron, and he hadn't said much except for that boring rubbish about aliens. It was like toys: when you brought them home from the shop and got them out of the box they were never quite the same. Life was full of disillusion.

'What'll we do about the tape?' asked Camille.

'Why should we do anything?' said Sam. 'We'll just leave it.'

'I think we should wipe it,' said Camille. 'It's sort of untidy somehow.'

'It's none of our business,' said Sam, 'and if we go round wiping her tapes, she'll know we've been here.'

'She'll know that anyway,' said Camille, 'on account of all the dirty dishes and the gâteau and stuff.'

'We're going to clean up later,' said Sam. 'When we get back from the pub.'

'But if she's dead,' said Camille, 'she wouldn't like that tape left lying around.'

'If she's dead,' said Sam, 'she's not going to mind much about anything, and anyway, if she went to all the trouble of making that tape in the first place, she's obviously not bothered about leaving it lying around. Besides . . .,' she added, 'she *can't* be dead.'

Camille had to agree that it did seem preposterous that anybody they had known should be dead. 'All the same,' she said, 'it's jolly odd.'

'The trouble with real villains,' said Constance, 'is they will tell lies. Terrible lies. Little villains aren't so bad.

They tell little lies to get themselves out of trouble or make themselves look good, but real villains live in a fantasy world. Some of them pretend they're the illegitimate sons of noblemen, and some of them pretend someone else did the murder. Sometimes they pretend they did the murder when they didn't, so's to alarm people. That always leads to trouble.'

'Why are you telling us this?' asked Brian.

'I was talking to Scarlet,' explained Constance. 'She was asking me about the criminal classes, so I was telling her.'

'Why do you have this interest in the criminal classes?' asked Brian of his wife.

'I was thinking about Barbs,' explained Scarlet.

'Barbs is hardly the criminal type,' said Clarissa.

'I never said she was,' said Scarlet. 'I was thinking she's the sort who encourages crime. She'll give a pound coin to one of the tinkers' children when there're dozens of them running round, and she'll let them see she's got lots more pound coins, and then she has to give them all one or they'll bang her on the head and take them.'

'You haven't got a very high opinion of human nature, have you?' remarked Clarissa.

'I suppose not,' said Scarlet. 'I don't see how I could have.'

'You need more faith,' said Clarissa. 'You should learn to trust people more.'

'Do what?' said Constance, her eyebrows high. 'You running for the council or something?'

'I beg your pardon?' said Clarissa, smiling.

'You sound like it,' said Constance. 'You sound as though you think the travellers are all good as gold if you're just a bit nice to them.'

'I'm sure that's true,' said Clarissa.

'I suppose it is, up to a point,' said Pam, 'but they've changed recently. They don't even sell white heather any more or tell your fortune. They just ask for money.'

'I think that's more honest,' said Clarissa.

'They're a damn nuisance,' said Brian, and Guy agreed.

'Are you suggesting that the travellers have murdered Barbs for her money?' asked Clarissa, ignoring this interruption from the men.

'I hadn't thought of that,' said Scarlet, 'but I suppose it's not impossible, when you come to think of it.'

'Or it might be one of the people they've turned out of the bins,' said Pam. 'The streets are full of madmen.'

'But the idea behind the policy was sound. Wasn't it, Guy?' said Clarissa.

Guy and Brian were discussing something of limited interest to women: something to do with commerce and the City. 'Sorry?' said Guy.

'It was wrong, wasn't it, to keep thousands of people locked up in those dreadful old Victorian institutions with no hope of release?' said Clarissa.

'Oh, undoubtedly,' said Guy.

'They got fed,' said Constance, 'and they had a roof over their heads. Not like what they've got to put up with now – ferreting round in the council bins for old take-aways and kipping in cardboard boxes. Me, I'd rather stay inside.'

'Some people can't bear being closed in,' said Clarissa. 'The travellers can't. They can't adjust to living in houses.'

'You can get used to it,' said Constance.

'Connie's family were all gipsies,' said Scarlet, because it was irresistible. She was taking a risk, for Constance sometimes rejoiced in her gipsy blood and sometimes deplored it. It all depended on her frame of mind.

'They still are,' said Constance. 'Mick sometimes takes

off in the wagon, but he's only too pleased to get back to Chigwell. He married an ordinary girl. My mother was wild at the time, but that was mostly because when Denise's family came to tea they used to lick the neck of the salad cream bottle.'

'Who's Denise?' asked Clarissa.

'Girl he married,' said Constance. 'She's improved a lot since then. Looks down on the needy and the greedy now.'

'Who?' asked Clarissa.

'The punters,' explained Constance. 'The ones Mick makes his money from – at the track.'

'The dog track,' said Scarlet. 'Connie's mum used to have winkles and celery for tea on Sunday,' she added, wistfully.

'We've got away from Barbs,' said Pam. 'We've forgotten about her again.'

Scarlet thought about Barbs. It seemed to happen all the time, even when she was present. She would be the centre of attention and then after a while you'd forget about her. Perhaps it was the same with everybody. No, it wasn't . . .

'Penny for them,' said Brian.

Scarlet took no notice and he assumed she hadn't heard him. She was bored. She tried to think what she'd rather be doing than sitting at the dinner table, and decided on sleep. They were all telling lies and lying was boring: that was why politicians were so boring, and clergymen and advertising copy-writers. Clarissa was enjoying moral indignation, while Pam was disguising her true feelings towards Clarissa. Brian was exaggerating his degree of success, and Guy, since he was eating Brian's salt, was affecting to believe him, while wearing a slight, incipient smile. Even Connie was wearing an untruthful dress, simpler than her usual garb, more suitable to a dinner-party: and when you came to think about it, Connie, at this dinner-party, was as incongruous as a rat. Brian was annoyingly right about that. This reflection led Scarlet to regret not that she had invited Connie but that she had invited the others. She would have had a much pleasanter evening alone with Con. 'Shall we go upstairs?' she said.

'I wonder what the girls are doing,' said Pam, as she rose and grappled about for her handbag.

'I expect they're fine,' said Scarlet, and she wasn't speaking the truth either. Perhaps that was a good sign; only the chronically unhappy and hopeless habitually spoke the truth, since the purpose of lying was to survive in one way or another, and the hopeless had no urge towards survival. 'I'll bring the coffee,' she said. 'Come and help me, Con.'

'That was good,' said Constance, brightly.

'I don't know why you're so cheerful,' said Scarlet. 'You've been cheerful all evening.'

'It's a front,' said Constance, 'but it wasn't a bad dinner – honestly.'

'You lie,' said Scarlet. 'It tasted like sawdust.'

'That's only because you cooked it,' said Connie. 'I mean you can't taste it properly because you cooked it not because you cooked sawdust.' Scarlet put out coffee cups and saucers and spoons, hating them as she did so. They reminded her of spoilt children – so small and precious, vulnerable and valuable and, practically speaking, useless.

'Shall I use mugs?' she asked.

'Yes,' said Constance, so Scarlet put the children back in the cupboard.

'I *am* going mad,' she said. 'I can feel it.'

'You're like the woman in that film I saw on Cable the other day,' said Constance. 'Her husband got rich and successful and adored her and gave her everything –

including one of those sod-awful American kids, but she liked it − and she was perfectly groomed and everyone loved her, so she took to the bottle.'

'There was probably more to it than met the eye,' said Scarlet.

'Less, if anything,' said Constance.

'Thanks,' said Scarlet.

'I don't mean you,' said Constance. 'You're awfully touchy these days.'

'No, I'm not,' said Scarlet. 'It's you. You're being *cheerful*. And you keep laughing.'

'I didn't laugh once,' said Constance. 'Not once.'

'Well, you looked as though you were,' said Scarlet. 'You looked as though you were going to out of sheer high spirits.'

'That was my *front*,' explained Constance, patiently. 'I'm crying inside, if you know what I mean.'

'Memet, I suppose,' said Scarlet.

'Memet,' agreed Constance. 'When I'm miserable I go on automatic and laugh more than usual.'

'What's he done now?' asked Scarlet.

'Nothing so far as I know. He hasn't been round.' Constance picked up the coffee pot. 'Shall we go?'

'You should ditch him and find someone else,' said Scarlet, offering Constance her own advice.

'Oh no,' said Constance, rejecting it. 'I haven't got time for that. You know how it goes − you find someone else and you have to start again. The last one's called Horace and likes his coffee black, then the next one's called Fred and he likes his coffee white, so you get them mixed up. Of course you do. Takes years getting it sorted out.'

'They all seem the same to me,' said Scarlet. 'More or less.'

'Well, they are mostly,' said Constance. 'But their mums gave them different prejudices, and they make different sorts of jokes, so you have to catch up on laughing at different things. And if the last one got you interested in opera, you have to forget all that if the next one's a Millwall supporter.'

'I wouldn't't've thought you'd worry about it,' said Scarlet.

'I don't much,' said Constance, 'but it's something else to trip you up on life's highway. Just one more damn thing. You don't want to hurt their feelings. Not unless you have to.'

'What are you girls doing?' came a cry from upstairs.

'What does he think we're doing?' muttered Scarlet.

'He probably thinks we're talking about him,' said Constance. 'They always think we're talking about them. They think we haven't got anything else to talk about.'

'We do talk about them a lot,' said Scarlet. 'Them or E additives. I think I'll go to night-school.'

There was a constrained atmosphere in the sitting-room, due mainly to Clarissa, who had her back to the others and was looking out of the window. 'She thinks she saw someone going into Barbs's house,' said Pam.

'It was probably Barbs,' said Constance. 'So that's all right then, isn't it?'

'It was a man,' said Clarissa.

'It's not unusual for men to go into Barbs's house,' said Constance.

Clarissa said nothing, but her stance expressed increasing disapproval. It was as though she were now convinced that Barbs was dead, and Clarissa adhered to the curious view that it was more reprehensible to speak ill of the dead – who, presumably, were past caring – than of the living who could be wounded by cruel rumours. She stood apart in a warm glow of moral indignation.

'Do you think I should go across and check?' asked Guy.

'I think we should ring the police,' said Clarissa.

'The last time I rang the police,' said Scarlet, 'they didn't come. There was a vagrant asleep on the doorstep and I couldn't get out of the house.'

'They come if you say you've seen a crime being committed,' said Brian.

'We haven't, have we?' said Constance. 'Have we seen a crime being committed?'

'The circumstances are suspicious,' said Clarissa. 'There's no point in waiting until somebody does something.'

'They won't come until somebody does,' said Constance. 'They're very firm about that. They won't come roaring out until somebody's done something. You can see their point. If they went flying round to every house every time someone saw somebody going in, they'd be exhausted.'

'It's no laughing matter,' said Guy.

'It's dead boring,' said Constance, 'if you want the truth.'

She seemed nervous, thought Scarlet idly, wondering why. 'Black or white?' she inquired generally.

'There's someone in the garden,' said Camille.

'You can't see the garden from here,' said Sam, who was making a desultory attempt at clearing up.

'I saw him go past the window,' said Camille, whispering now.

'Where?' asked Tim, in the aggressive tones of the householder.

'Don't shout,' said Camille. 'I'm frightened . . .'

'Don't you be so pathetic,' said Sam. 'What you got to be frightened of?'

'If you don't know,' began Camille, fear beginning to be ousted by annoyance, 'I don't see why I should waste my time telling you. It might be anyone – Barbs or the police, or a mad axe-man, or anyone.'

'Probably just one of the tramps,' said Sam, 'looking for somewhere to sleep.'

'I'll go and see,' said Tim.

'Don't be stupid,' said Camille, and after a moment they saw the point of her reservations. The territorial instinct which had been aroused in Tim faded as he remembered that they had no right to be where they were, any more than anyone else.

'What'll we do?' he asked.

'Keep down,' said Sam, dropping to the floor. The boy from the bistro, being used to finding himself in bizarre circumstances, did likewise. Sam thought, with brief regret, that the evening was certainly not turning out as she had planned, and then, remembering that things seldom did, she ceased to worry about it. 'I'm going to go to the back door and look out,' she announced.

Camille sat down behind the sofa and Joe stretched himself on the rug.

'What can you see?' demanded Tim, crawling to where Sam was crouched by the French windows. The bottom panel was made of wood, and she had to raise herself on her knees to peer out.

'Nothing,' she said, 'only bits of trees and grass. He must've gone. If he was ever there,' she added, irritably, 'and Cam wasn't seeing things.' She got up and pressed her face against the second pane of glass. Simultaneously someone came round the side of the house and peered in. He and Sam looked straight into each other's eyes, for Sam was tall for a girl. 'You frightened me,' she accused, as she opened the door.

'So did you me,' said Memet. 'What are you doing?'

'I think I'm going to die,' said Sam. 'I never had such a fright in my life.'

'Nor did I,' said Memet. 'I'll never have children now.' His mother held that a sudden shock could render a man sterile.

'What were you doing out there?' demanded Sam.

'I asked first,' said Memet. 'What's going on?'

'I'm having a dinner-party,' said Sam, with dignity, beginning to revive. Memet, although an adult, was not one of the enemy. Basically, he was not respectable and could therefore be trusted. 'So now I've told you what we're doing, what were *you* doing?'

'I came for my hat,' said Memet. 'I left it here.'

Camille came into the kitchen. 'I nearly died of fright when I heard you talking,' she said. 'My heart won't stop beating. You nearly frightened me to death.'

'If your heart did stop beating, you'd be dead,' said Sam, who had regained her equanimity. 'Don't be such a chicken.'

'Why are you having your dinner-party here?' inquired Memet. He had retrieved his hat from the window-sill and was wearing it.

'Why d'you think?' said Sam. 'Our mothers wouldn't let us have one at home, that's why!'

'What would Barbs say?' asked Memet.

'She's dead,' said an unexpected voice. Joe had joined them. He had started on the gâteau and his mouth was full, so that his utterance lacked conviction.

Everyone started speaking at once.

'Be quiet,' shouted Memet. 'What are you talking about?' he asked as they fell silent. 'You.' He pointed at Joe.

Joe looked round – a bit dopily, thought Sam. 'I've

gathered,' said Joe, 'that the lady who lives in this house is dead.'

They all started talking again.

'She's left her make-up,' yelled Sam, 'so we thought she must be dead. Otherwise she wouldn't've. I didn't think you were taking any notice,' she said, resentfully, addressing Joe.

'I could hardly help it,' said Joe. 'It was interesting.'

'Yes, well, just don't go telling people,' said Camille. 'It's none of your business.'

'If you want to know what I think,' said Tim, 'I think we should clear up and clear out of here before anything else happens. Before we're caught.'

'We haven't done anything,' said Sam.

'Breaking and entering,' ventured Tim. 'Aggravated burglary, using a person's gas and electricity and tap water and table linen without her permission, poking around on her premises, listening to her tapes . . .'

'What tapes?' asked Memet.

'Oh, just some tapes,' said Tim shiftily. 'Nothing in particular.'

'I think I'd better have a look around,' said Memet.

'Why?' asked Sam. 'We've had a look round already.' Something in Memet's demeanour nettled her. He was behaving rather like her mother; he was beginning almost to *bustle*, as though she couldn't be relied upon to do anything by herself, as though whatever conclusions she had drawn must be verified by someone of greater age, integrity and intelligence. As though she were incompetent. 'We found her handbag and her make-up and she hasn't made her bed. She's *dead*.' Sam regretted having put it so emphatically when she heard herself, for death was a matter of some significance, and she had to admit that a mature and responsible person would be bound to mention it to the authorities. 'What you going to do about it?' she demanded, truculently.

'Me?' said Memet. 'I'm not going to do anything. Why should I?' He looked rather pale, and Sam thought she must have given him a bigger shock than she'd realized.

'Oh, sorry,' she said. 'I thought you were going rushing off to Holmes Road.'

'Don't be silly,' said Memet, absently. He wandered into the sitting-room.

'We might as well tidy up now,' said Tim, 'before we go out. I don't somehow like the idea of coming back later. It could be asking for trouble.'

'Oh, all right,' said Sam. 'You'll have to wash up in the dark or strike matches or something.'

'What do you mean – *I*'ll have to wash up?' said Tim. 'I made the dressing and the sauce . . .'

'Don't argue,' said Camille. 'We'll all do it.' She had a natural ability to tidy up and restore order, but since this was not a glamorous or interesting characteristic, she kept it concealed from her friends, thinking of it in her more depressed moments as something that might come in useful one day if all else failed. No one, seeing her room, would ever have suspected its existence.

'You feeling all right?' asked Sam incredulously.

'Don't start or you'll put me off the idea,' said Camille. 'We've got to tidy up or they might think we murdered her.' While not following her reasoning, Sam agreed that it might be wise to eliminate all trace of their occupation.

As she washed the plates in cold water Camille thought about the kennels. It had occurred to her earlier that if Constance had learned that Memet had had sexual intercourse with Barbs, she might have chopped her up and given the pieces to her brother to cook in his huge pot for his dogs. She envisaged the scene in her mind: 'Here, Mick, give me a hand, will you?' 'What is it, Con?' 'Help me get these bits of Barbs out of the back of the motor. I want you to boil her for me.' 'Sure, Con. Anything for you. How'd you like her done, medium or rare?' 'I don't know, Mick. Any way the dogs'd like her. I leave it to you.' 'OK, Con.' Camille was quite lost in this fantasy, puzzling out the practical problems posed by the disposal of the human head in particular. It would have to be cut in half, or into unrecognizable quarters, and boiled until the flesh just fell away. She wondered if greyhounds were permitted to use their valuable feet to dig holes and bury bones.

'Will you let me get at the sink, Cam?' said Sam. 'I've asked you three times.'

'I was thinking,' said Camille.

'What about?' asked Sam. 'What's so interesting it's made you think?'

'Nothing much,' said Camille. The child that she was wanted to share the story with Sam, who would, if she hadn't grown too old in the presence of the boy from the bistro, have ideas of her own to contribute. The adult, however, whom she was soon to become, frowned upon this inclination: it was all very well for children to make things up because no one believed them. When grown-ups did it, even if they were pathological liars or raving mad, the tendency was to listen to them and, possibly, even take their words at face value. She sighed. The days when she and Sam made up stories together had passed and a lifetime of boring reality lay ahead. If she spoke about the dogs' dinner, she could easily get Connie into trouble because, outwardly at least, Camille knew she now looked like a grown person who should perhaps be taken seriously. She thought she would have to go and live abroad and learn a new language to bring some interest into her life: otherwise, by some dread mischance, she might end up like her mother, washing dishes for ever and always telling the truth except when it would be obviously inadvisable. She was confused by a conviction that it was more sound to stick to the truth and a yearning for the bright and coloured realms of fantasy. Then for a moment she was overwhelmed by a knowledge of the reality of death: the dead Barbs of her imagining might be a truly dead Barbs, which would not be nearly so amusing.

'Why're you looking as though someone had pinched your bum?' demanded Sam.

'I just thought one of those things you usually only wake up in the night and think,' said Camille. 'It was so *nasty*.'

'Well, forget about that and let's get out,' said Sam. Camille put the plates in the cupboard and the cutlery into the drawer. 'It looks tidier now than when we got here,' observed Sam, approvingly. 'You surprise me sometimes, Camille.'

'I'm not thick,' said Camille, crossly. 'I do know how to wash up.'

'But you don't often do it,' said Sam. Camille ignored her.

'We'd better go out the back way,' said Tim. 'I'll put my hand through the hole in the window and lock the door and put the thingy back.'

'Come on, you,' said Sam to the boy from the bistro, whom she had gone off.

'Where's what's-'is-face?' asked Tim. Memet came downstairs.

'What've you been doing?' asked Sam accusingly.

Memet became increasingly authoritarian. 'I've been checking that you kids haven't messed the place up,' he said. 'You might have got into terrible trouble doing what you've done tonight. I've been making sure you haven't left any cigarette ends lying about to start a fire or any windows open to let burglars in.'

Sam was furious when he said this. The voice on the tape might have been his, and if it was, he had absolutely no right to tick them off about anything. Not after what he'd been doing. Unfortunately, he was too old for her to start screaming at him, nor did she know him well enough. She turned her back on him and made for the garden door, holding her dignified head high.

'What about the tapes?' asked Tim.

'What about them?' said Sam, scornfully.

'They've gone,' said Camille, from the back of the room. 'They're not here.'

'You must've put them somewhere,' said Tim.

'I never . . .,' began Camille.

'Oh, forget the bloody tapes,' said Sam. 'Let's just get out.'

'Yes, quickly,' said Memet. 'You don't want to be found here.' He was wearing one hat and carrying another. 'I'll go first,' he said. 'Make sure no one sees you leaving.'

'I don't trust that man,' said Sam, as they stood around the snooker table at the Elephant's Head.

'Why should you?' asked Camille. 'Why should *you* trust him? He's Connie's one.'

'If I was her, I wouldn't trust him either,' said Sam.

'Are we going to play snooker or are you going to stand round arguing all night?' asked Tim.

'I'm going home,' said Sam, who had started on the path of disenchantment.

'Actually, me too,' said Camille, pleased that her friend no longer fancied bistro Joe. 'I'm starving.'

'Where have you been?' asked Scarlet. She had heard Camille letting herself in and had gone into the hallway to make sure that this was indeed her daughter returned.

'With Sam,' said Camille.

'But where?' said Scarlet.

'Just around,' said Camille. 'Does it matter?' Pam came out to join them.

'Where's Sam?' she asked.

Camille foresaw an interrogation and yawned. 'I'm tired,' she said. 'Sam's at home.'

'What is she doing?' demanded Sam's mother.

'Nothing,' said Camille.

'I suppose that's normal,' said Pam. 'I never know whether it's worse when she's doing nothing or when she's doing something.'

Camille thought how difficult to please all parents were, but she could see that both mothers were so relieved to know where their respective daughters were that they would not now concern themselves with rebukes.

'So you didn't have a party in my house?' asked Pam.

'No,' said Camille. 'Good night.'

'I wonder what they've been up to?' said Scarlet.

'It's just as well we don't know,' said Pam. 'I always try and remember that when I find myself wondering.'

'It's time I went home,' said Constance. She had been standing by the window drinking her coffee and had the impression that she had just seen Memet walk out of Barbs's gate and down the street: she knew she could have been mistaken, being entirely familiar with the derangement which leads the lover to see the beloved in all manner of unexpected circumstances, but she wanted to go and make sure. Sadly, she could not just put down her cup and leap from the house, so she finished her coffee, made her farewells and left with as much haste as was seemly.

'What did you say to Connie?' asked Scarlet of her husband.

'I didn't say anything,' said Brian.

'She left awfully quickly,' said Scarlet, suspiciously.

'You know Connie,' said Clarissa, smiling indulgently. Scarlet wanted to say that of course she knew Connie, she knew Connie better than anyone else did, and that this precipitate departure was uncharacteristic of her, but she stayed silent, since she could not express her feelings without sounding foolish and presenting Connie in a bad light. If she said that Connie was usually the last to leave, it would seem that Connie must, on this occasion, have taken offence at something, and Scarlet considered that people who took offence at things that were said in other people's houses were exhibiting the worst of bad manners. While she knew that Connie would not be upset by any remark of Brian's she also knew that she found him and his conversation tedious, but she could not accuse her husband of boring her guest into leaving any more than she could openly accuse him of discourtesy. Scarlet was annoyed. She remembered an occasion when Barbs had risen from the dinner table and left in the middle of the soup because somebody had made a disparaging remark about queers. Scarlet had never forgiven Barbs for that. 'I wonder if Barbs is back yet?' she said.

'Is there a light in her house?' asked Clarissa. Scarlet went to the window and looked across the street.

'No,' she said, 'but I thought I saw one earlier when I let the cat in. It might've been the house next door, though. They're so close together.'

153

'We'll call and see on our way home,' said Clarissa. 'I feel guilty I haven't done something before. Barbs would never have left it this long if she thought anything had happened to one of us.'

'No, she wouldn't, would she?' said Scarlet. You only had to sneeze to have Barbs coming round with hot lemon juice and concerned inquiries as to your health. If you looked miserable, Barbs wouldn't rest until she'd questioned you to the point of exhaustion, with particular reference to your love life. She was an awful woman, thought Scarlet, released by her neighbour's protracted absence from the need to give her the benefit of the doubt. She was, reflected Scarlet, indeed very similar to those people whom Constance fled from. The ones who called at the door to tell you how much the Lord loved you and ask what you were doing about it. When they were there, you felt bad because you were being unresponsive. It was only when they'd gone that you realized how loathsome they were.

'You said that as though you didn't believe it,' said Guy.

'Said what?' asked Scarlet, who was thinking vengefully of the times Barbs had helped her out.

'You said Barbs wouldn't wait before she started worrying about one of us,' said Clarissa, 'but you sounded as though you didn't believe it.'

'I believe it all right,' said Scarlet. They were nonplussed at this and shortly afterwards left, claiming to have had a delightful evening.

'I don't understand you,' said Brian. 'You've never really liked Barbs, yet you put up with Constance. It doesn't make sense.'

'Oh, Brian,' said Scarlet, 'can't you see?'

'See what?' demanded Brian, pursuing her upstairs. He was at the argumentative stage of intoxication.

'It doesn't matter,' said Scarlet.

'Yes, it does,' persisted Brian. 'I want to know what you see in Constance and why you don't like Barbs. Are you jealous of her?'

Scarlet was astonished. 'Of *Barbs*?' she said, incredulously.

'I don't know why you say it like that,' said Brian. 'She's a very attractive woman.'

'She's hell,' said Scarlet, sitting down on the bed and taking off a shoe.

'A lot of men round here wouldn't agree with you,' said Brian. 'I think that's it. I think you're jealous of her.'

It was not the first time that Scarlet had been forced to notice the vast disparity between the male and the female view of female attractiveness. 'You're such a fool,' she said, and this did represent a first time. She thought how odd it was that the men of the district should admire Barbs, who appeared to fly the feminist flag and should have spent her time putting them in their place. It seemed that instead of being alarmed they saw her as not too different from themselves, something of a tomboy who reassuringly shared the view that the sex act was no big deal: a woman free of coy inhibition must be a gratifying gift to the male, no matter what she herself thought her motives might be. Silly bitch, thought Scarlet. Constance said she couldn't stand feminists because they reminded her of men. Just as if there weren't enough of *them* around already.

Brian went to sleep in the spare room and Scarlet was further astonished to discover how relieved she was, how pleasant it was not to lie beside an offended body as it breathed loudly and tensed its muscles in rebuke. She stretched over the bed and slept until the following morning.

★

Camille was up extraordinarily early and had eaten a bowl of cornflakes and a strawberry-flavoured yoghurt before her mother came down. 'Mum,' she said.

'Yes, darling,' said Scarlet.

'Mum,' said Camille again.

'Yes,' said Scarlet, patiently. 'Don't go on saying "Mum", there's a good girl.'

'Yes, well – Mum,' said Camille.

'What?' said Scarlet.

'Mum, what are you going to do about Barbs?'

'Not you too,' said Scarlet. 'Nobody seems to think about anything but Barbs these days.'

Camille made herself a piece of toast and put jam on it.

'Not too much butter,' said Scarlet, automatically. 'Why are you so worried about Barbs?'

'I'm not,' said Camille, hurriedly. 'Not really.'

Her mother wondered if this was another manifestation of her daughter's budding sense of social responsibility. Only a few weeks before she had arrived home in tears because she had stood behind an old man in the check-out counter at Sainsbury's: he had been trying to buy a carton of milk and a packet of biscuits and had found he had no money. Brian had suggested that he probably did it all the time in the hope that some mug would come across with the readies, and Camille had yelled that she had tried to give the old man money and he wouldn't take it. She had called her stepfather, among other things, a mean pillock. At the time Scarlet had thought that her period was probably due.

'I know what you mean, darling,' she said, 'but if Barbs has just gone on holiday for a few days, she wouldn't thank us for making a fuss.'

'Yes, she would,' said Camille. 'She likes people making a fuss about her.'

There was a pause as Scarlet readjusted her ideas of her daughter's mental age and degree of perspicacity. 'True,' she said, carefully, 'but we don't want to make idiots of ourselves, bothering the police about nothing, do we?'

'No,' said Camille, reaching for an apple.

'Rinse it under the tap,' said Scarlet.

'She might be murdered,' said Camille.

Scarlet, who was still herself toying with this notion, dismissed it. 'Nonsense,' she said.

'It's no good saying "nonsense",' said Camille, 'There's been three murders round here since last Saturday. I know it's mostly people outside pubs pulling knives, but people murder people.'

'I do wish you wouldn't go into pubs,' said Scarlet, her terrors reactivated. 'You're years under-age anyway.'

'Oh, Mum,' said Camille, 'I only drink Coke,' she added, mendaciously.

'I don't know what to do,' said Scarlet. 'I'll ask Connie again what she thinks.'

'Maybe Connie murdered her,' said Camille.

Scarlet jumped. 'Don't say things like that,' she said. 'You could make awful trouble. How can you say things like that about Connie?'

'I wouldn't blame her,' said Camille. 'Barbs is a prat.' Scarlet couldn't think what to say next. It looked as though she and her daughter would, before very long, be in accord about several matters: she had despaired of ever seeing the day, and now it was approaching she felt a vague sense of anticlimax. Somehow, when Camille was younger, Scarlet had hoped and believed that she would grow up wiser and cleverer than herself, would develop into a brilliant and glorious human being, for babies and small children seem implicit with this improbable promise. Even the awe-inspiring monster that Camille had become in adolescence had been different in its very horror, but now it looked as though she was becoming like her mother in her responses and attitudes. Scarlet thought this would make her ordinary. It all seemed disappointingly pointless.

'Now you're growing up so fast,' she said, 'perhaps you should do something about Barbs – if you're really worried.'

'No way,' said Camille.

Scarlet was perversely reassured. 'Let's leave it a bit longer,' she said, 'and see what happens.' Brian came into the kitchen wearing the expression of the insulted male. Oh, God, thought Scarlet. 'Would you like an egg?' she inquired.

'No, thanks,' said Brian. He made himself a cup of tea and drank it as he assembled the contents of his briefcase. Then he left.

'What's up with him?' asked Camille.

'I upset him,' said Scarlet, shortly.

'What's so funny,' said Camille, 'is the way when they're mad they won't eat – as though eating was doing you a favour.'

Perhaps, thought Scarlet, her child was growing up to resemble not herself but Connie: that had been the sort of insight to which Connie was given. The possibility cheered her.

'Hurry up or you'll be late for school,' she said.

'It's only a study period first thing,' said Camille, who had no intention of going to school

She wandered down to the canal and watched some ducks floating busily about. Already the Lock area was filled with tourists, who came from all over the world to visit this insalubrious spot. Camille regarded them with contempt, hitching herself up to sit on a bit of wedge-shaped wall beside the footpath which bordered the canal. The wall was on the other side, jutting over a still and lifeless backwater which was partly concealed by the surrounding buildings and looked even more dangerously filthy than the canal itself. She waited for Tim.

'You know what?' she said, when he arrived.

'No, what?' he said.

'That voice,' she said, 'that man's voice on Barbs's tape – d'you know who it sounded like?'

'No, who?' asked Tim, who was eating a packet of nuts and spitting the shells into the water.

'My stepfather,' said Camille.

'Nuts,' said Tim.

'Not at the moment,' said Camille.

'You know what I mean,' said Tim.

'Yes, I know what you mean,' said Camille. 'Only it did. It sounded just like him.'

'You're only saying that because you *don't* like him,' said Tim.

'I know,' said Camille, 'but wouldn't it be fun if it was?'

'Not for your mum,' said Tim.

'She'd get used to it,' said Camille, 'and if you're going to be Christian, I'm going away.'

'You couldn't tell who it was,' said Tim, 'not doing that. It could be anybody.'

'How disgusting,' said Camille. 'How disgusting if it could be anybody.'

'You're very young for your age,' said Tim. 'It's time . . .'

'If you're going to say I should meet your friend Chris,' said Camille, 'I'll push you in the water.'

'I wasn't,' said Tim. 'I was going to say it was time you started to grow up.'

'I don't want to grow up at the moment,' said Camille. 'Just look at them – those are grown-ups taking photographs of the shitty old canal.'

'Those are tourists,' said Tim. 'You have to make allowances.'

'You're being Christian,' wailed Camille.

'I was joking,' said Tim. 'Don't you know when someone's joking?'

'I can't tell with you,' said Camille. 'You always sound the same. I think your timing's wrong.' She glanced at him sideways to see if he would take offence at this, but he looked as he usually did, placid and cheerful. 'You're not very grown-up either,' she said. 'You don't behave like a man.'

'You don't know many men,' said Tim. 'You've had very limited experience and you can't form any proper judgements yet.'

'Oh, la-di-da,' said Camille, in her grandmother's voice. 'This canal smells. Let's go to the bar.'

'I've got to go to school later,' said Tim.

Camille was instantly overwhelmed by *tedium vitae*. 'So what'll I do?' she demanded.

'How about going to school too?' suggested Tim. 'They're going to catch you out sooner or later.'

'Then they'll have to send me to a crammer,' said Camille. 'I could go to Sam's one. They don't teach you anything at my school. They don't even try,' she added, as Tim opened his mouth to speak. 'And the girls are all slags.'

'So tell your mother,' said Tim, 'explain to her.'

'I did,' said Camille. 'Brian says he might send me to a crammer. He'll think about it.'

'There you are, then,' said Tim. 'I told you he wasn't all bad.'

'If I don't go on about it, he'll forget,' said Camille. 'I have to go on and on before they listen to me. They don't really care about me at all. They only care about themselves.' Tim didn't say anything. 'It's no good you saying I'm childish,' Camille went on, 'I know Mum loves me. I know she worries about me, but she doesn't *think* about me. Not really *me*.'

'Why should she, really?' asked Tim. 'She isn't you. Only you're you. That's why you have to grow up – so you can think for yourself.'

'You've been doing philosophy or something,' said Camille. 'It's made you awfully boring.'

'I just thought of that,' protested Tim, 'and what's more, I think it's true.'

'Oh, maybe,' said Camille, 'maybe you're right. I don't know. I'm just fed up.'

Scarlet would have recognized her daughter's mood. She was feeling somewhat similar and had left the confines of the house to sit in the garden and shell peas, an action which throughout history had been a good and a womanly thing to do.

'Coming shopping?' asked Constance, leaning on the fence.

'Why did you leave so early last night?' asked Scarlet in return. 'Was it Clarissa?'

'No, no,' said Constance. 'I thought I saw Memet sneaking about, so I went to have a look, but he'd gone.'

'I thought you couldn't stand us any longer,' said Scarlet.

'That's your inferiority complex,' said Constance, '*and* you're agoraphobic. I've been reading a DIY psychiatry book. You don't need that therapist any more. You got me.'

'I'm giving her up anyway,' said Scarlet. 'If we send Camille to a crammer, we won't be able to afford her.'

'Good,' said Constance. 'Shops?'

'I suppose so,' said Scarlet. 'I might as well. We could do with some more Persil and things.'

'I've decided to give up Memet,' said Constance. 'I've been losing sleep over him and it won't do. Trouble is I can't find him to tell him so.'

'He'll be round,' said Scarlet.

The streets and shops were crowded with the indigenous population, merging, as they neared the Lock, with the visiting sightseers. 'I remember round here when there was proper shops,' said Constance. 'You could buy things you needed. Now all you can buy is beads and mirrors.'

'You sell beads,' said Scarlet.

'Yes, well, I'm not silly, am I?' said Constance. 'If that's what they want, that's what I'll sell them.'

'I remember too,' said Scarlet. 'I remember when there were little grocers' shops and ironmongers' and a place where they mended brass things.'

'There's plenty of those left,' said Constance.

'They're not the same,' said Scarlet.

'There was a pie-and-mash shop up there,' said Constance.

'And a place down there where they made their own sausages,' said Scarlet. 'Proper ones that burst in the pan.'

'And a horrible murder happened just here,' said Constance. 'Outside this pub.'

'They still happen,' said Scarlet, determined not to suppress her anxiety.

'Not the same,' said Constance. 'Murder's got no glamour now. Not since they sacked the hangman.'

'If Barbs is murdered,' said Scarlet, 'once upon a time they'd have hanged somebody for it.'

'If they could've caught him,' said Constance. 'It wouldn't've been fair, though. Barbs went round asking to be murdered.'

'It's funny you should say that,' said Scarlet. 'I was thinking just the same thing the other day. I never realized how much I didn't like her until she wasn't there. I suppose if she doesn't turn up soon, we'll have to do something about it – tell the police or the social services or somebody.'

'It's my belief,' said Constance, 'she's doing it on purpose to get herself noticed.' She stopped, so suddenly that Scarlet walked into her. 'Sorry,' she said. 'I thought I saw someone.'

'Not Barbs,' said Scarlet.

'No,' said Constance.

That night Memet returned. He let himself in, humming what was presumably a Turkish air. Constance didn't recognize it, but she knew his step and the smell of his after-shave.

'So you're back,' she said, spitting out a bead, which she had been holding in her mouth for safe-keeping. She put down the necklace she was threading and turned to look at him.

'I haven't been away,' he said.

'You haven't been here,' said Constance.

'Only for a day or so,' said Memet. 'It hasn't been long. It only seems so to you when you miss me so terribly.'

'I haven't missed you at all,' said Constance. 'I've been run off my feet.'

'Doing what?' inquired Memet.

'This and that,' said Constance. 'What do you want?' These words caused Memet to realize that the evening that

lay ahead would not be comfortable: they held the unmistakable implication – state your business and go. It was
probable, judging by her tone, that he would not be spending the evening with Constance. He took off his hat with
deliberate lack of haste and stood looking at her. Constance
looked at his hat: it was the straw one she had last seen on
Barbs's window-sill.

'I brought some Johnny Walker,' said Memet, proffering
the bottle. Constance hesitated; she could just do with a
drop of scotch.

'You know where the glasses are,' she said, sliding another bead on to her necklace.

'That's pretty,' said Memet. 'I like that one. It's really
pretty.'

'Do leave off,' said Constance.

'I meant it,' said Memet, removing his jacket.

'Make yourself at home,' said Constance, but he sensed
the worst was over. She was silent while he poured the
whisky, concentrating on her craft.

'So, what've you been up to?' asked Memet, sitting
down on the sofa, but not yet putting his feet on it: he was
prepared to be careful.

'Just the usual,' said Constance, 'Work, work and more
work.' Memet didn't classify stringing beads as work but
did not say so.

'I've been on the road,' said Constance, untruthfully. 'I
have to make a crust and it's better than going on the
streets.' Memet laughed, insincerely and for too long. He
sounded like a man with an uneasy conscience. 'It wasn't
really funny,' said Constance, stringing more beads.

'I laugh when I'm happy,' said Memet.

'You don't usually,' said Constance. 'I don't seem to
remember you hooting like that. You sound potty.'

164

'I've had a lot to worry me, said Memet, changing his tune.

'You're going to tell me times are hard. You're going to say you've been hit by the recession,' said Constance. 'You're going to tell me you've had to start drawing on the Swiss bank.'

'I had some losses,' said Memet.

'You shouldn't bet,' said Constance.

'Business losses,' said Memet.

'Huh,' said Constance. The silence grew prolonged.

'Why are you so quiet?' inquired Memet. 'Are you annoyed about something?'

'The jury's still out on that one,' said Constance, shortly. 'Further evidence may be called for.'

'I don't like you like this,' said Memet.

'How unfortunate,' said Constance.

'I'll take you out to dinner,' he said, as one inspired.

'No, you won't,' said Constance.

'I'll go then,' said Memet, rising.

'Fine by me,' said Constance, biting through a thread.

'Ow, Connie, you shouldn't do that,' said Memet. 'You'll break your teeth.' He was moved by genuine concern for her incisors, since he was only one generation away from the blackened and carious stumps of his peasant ancestry and had an almost American reverence for orthodontics. Constance took it as concern for her welfare, her overall well-being, and was mollified.

'Oh, sit down,' she said, 'and take that silly hat off.'

'I *have* been busy,' said Memet.

'Yeah, yeah,' said Constance, but she spoke patiently now, rather than sardonically. 'I'll have another scotch,' she said, and pushed her beads aside.

When the evening had mellowed and the whisky was

low in the bottle, Memet said in an enticing, placatory voice reminiscent of Eliot's that he had something to confess.

Constance sat upright. 'I don't want to know,' she said. 'I don't care,' and she meant it, for if he felt able to tell her what he had been up to, then either it was too trivial to be of any significance or he minded not at all about her emotional susceptibilities. Either way it was oddly insulting. For a crazed moment Constance thought that the only truth worth hearing was that which you beat out of people, that which had to be delved and probed for, for few people offered freely anything of any value. 'Keep your old confession to yourself,' she said.

Memet, as was more or less usual, misunderstood her. 'You don't understand,' he said. 'I didn't have an affair with that woman. I killed her.'

'If you said what I think you just said,' remarked Constance, amiably, 'I'm glad I didn't have any beads in my mouth because I'd've swallowed them. What do you mean, you killed her?'

'I killed her,' said Memet, and he stroked his shirt collar.

'Are you telling me you cut her throat or throttled her, or what?' demanded Constance.

'No,' said Memet, disdainfully. 'Don't be vulgar.'

'You thought up something classier, did you?' said Constance. 'Like what? And don't try showing off to me because I know you too well.'

'It was an accident,' said Memet, moderately, and Constance thought her heart stopped. It sounded like the truth and she wished it unsaid. She wished he had claimed to have thrown Barbs out of an aeroplane, so that she could have disbelieved him.

'Did anybody see you?' she asked, dry-mouthed.

'No, of course not,' said Memet.

For a moment she thought she would leave it there, not ask any more, but that would have been worse than knowing. 'You'd better tell me about it,' she said.

'It was nothing really,' said Memet. 'We had an argument and I pushed her and she fell in.'

'Fell in what?' said Constance. 'What argument? Will you just start at the beginning?'

'I met her by the canal,' said Memet, 'and she was sitting on the wall, and I gave her a little push and walked away and when I looked back she wasn't there.'

'Did you see her fall in? Did you hear her?' asked Constance.

'No,' admitted Memet. 'But she'd gone.'

'So she probably got down and walked home,' said Constance. 'You *are* showing off. I wish you wouldn't.'

'But she isn't at home,' said Memet. 'Is she?'

'What were you arguing about then?' said Constance, courageously, for she could only think of lovers' tiffs.

'About you,' said Memet. 'She said some things about you, so I smacked her.' This, while gratifying, was unconvincing.

'Try again,' said Constance, 'harder this time.'

'It's true,' said Memet. 'She didn't like you. She'd've got you into trouble if she could. She was jealous of you.'

'Why?' asked Constance flatly.

'Not what you think,' said Memet. 'You were like what she wanted to be like, only you were really like it. That's all.' It made a sort of sense. Constance was rather impressed by his percipience.

'So why was your hat hanging up in her house?' she inquired.

'I left it there,' said Memet with the brazen expression of one preparing himself to be justly accused.

'And what were you doing there? Ticking her off for being disrespectful about me again, were you?'

'I was trying to borrow money,' said Memet.

Sometimes he took her breath away. She told him so.

'She was loaded,' said Memet. 'Didn't you know?'

'No,' said Constance, but that, too, made sense. Barbs, as far as anyone knew, had never worked and lived, if not lavishly, yet well. 'Trust you to know that,' she said, unfairly, since she could have reached the same conclusion herself if she'd thought about it.

'What did you think she lived on?' asked Memet.

'I didn't think,' said Constance. 'I am not, by nature, an inquisitive person.'

'That was another reason she didn't like you,' said Memet.

'I can see that,' said Constance. 'Nosy people always think people who aren't nosy are stuck-up.' She dwelt on this aspect of human nature for a while.

'She might be that body they pulled out,' said Memet.

'It hadn't got any identifying things on it,' said Constance, 'so unless we go and have a look — and I don't propose we do — we'll never know.'

'Her handbag's in her house,' said Memet. 'With all her cards and everything.'

'I'm not going to ask how you know that,' said Constance, after another silence, 'because I don't think I want to know.'

'It was those kids,' said Memet. 'Camo and the other one — they were having a party in Barbs's house. I saw signs of life and I thought she'd come back, so I went to see, and it was only the kids snooping round and messing up the kitchen.' He sounded disapproving.

'At least they hadn't murdered the householder,' said Constance. 'I never know when to believe you or not.'

'I *saw* them there,' said Memet.

'I mean about pushing women in canals,' said Constance.

'Would I say I had if I hadn't?' asked Memet.

'You might,' said Constance, 'or you might be genuinely mistaken. Why were you trying to borrow money?' It wasn't as silly a question as it sounded. Memet was reluctant to answer: his moment of honesty had passed, leaving him at a loss. He hadn't needed money, not desperately, but he liked to know he could persuade women to part with it. Whatever he now told Constance would not put him in a good light, and he was unaware that she did not see him in a good light anyway. 'I suppose it's just your nature,' she said.

'Like a little child with his nose to a sweetshop window,' said Memet, affectionately.

'I meant greedy, thieving and disgusting,' corrected Constance without animosity, for she could overlook these characteristics in a lover who was not blatantly unfaithful, although they would serve as excuses for dismissing him should his faithlessness go to unacceptable lengths. She felt calm now, since even if Memet had murdered Barbs, it had not been a crime of passion, and it seemed he had not been observed. Constance did not subscribe to the view that murder will out, knowing from second-hand experience and hearsay that this was not the case. If Memet was indeed guilty, it was faintly worrying that he had felt impelled to confess to her, but she did not think that he was the conscience-ridden type who would make a habit of it. She had too much sense to agonize over what was done; and it was still perfectly possible that it had not been done at all. She would not tell Scarlet about this, for Scarlet idolized her and might mistakenly believe that it was her duty to report her lover to the police. She couldn't be bothered to explain. 'Well, never mind,' she said.

★

'Connie saw me yesterday,' said Camille.

'I thought she saw you most days,' said Sam.

'Down the High Street,' said Camille, 'when I should've been in school.'

'She won't tell your mum, will she?' asked Sam.

'No, of course she won't,' said Camille. 'Connie doesn't grass.'

'Then what are you worrying about?' said Sam, yawning.

'It gave me a shock,' said Camille, who shared the belief in personal invisibility held by all petty wrongdoers. People intent on breaking into banks take precautions not to be recognized, while those engaged in more minor misdemeanours take it for granted that they will not be noticed. It seems unfair of fate when they are. 'I was lucky Mum didn't see me,' she said. 'I suppose they were doing the shopping.'

'People do,' said Tim, idly.

'It was a coincidence they were there the same time as me, though,' said Camille, aggrieved. They were leaning against their favoured stretch of wall on the bridge over the evil-smelling depths of the canal backwater. 'If you pushed someone in here,' she said, 'would they float out again, d'you suppose?'

'Shouldn't think so,' said Sam. 'Why should they?'

'Currents?' suggested Camille.

'It's stagnant,' said Tim, 'but after a week or two they get full of gas and bob up, unless there's something holding them down.'

'How do they get full of gas?' inquired Sam, perhaps with dim memories of camping holidays, canisters and stoves.

'They decompose,' said Tim, 'and it forms gases in

them.' Camille leaned further over the wall, looking for signs of this phenomenon, but all she could see was floating packaging, crisp packets, condoms, burger boxes and other evidence of the consumer society's indulgences.

'There's only a load of crud,' she said.

'You die of disease if you fall in anyway,' said Sam.

'We shouldn't be wasting our youth here,' said Tim.

'Hallelujah,' said Camille. 'He's doing it again.'

'I wasn't,' said Tim. 'I was thinking of the health risk.'

'You sounded Christian to me,' said Camille.

'Connie's religious,' said Sam, merely to annoy.

'No, she's not,' said Camille contrarily.

'You said she was, and she goes to church,' said Sam.

'But she doesn't go round *being* it,' said Camille. 'Not so you want to push her in the canal. Not like the Archbishop of Canterbury here.'

'You shouldn't be so mean to him,' said Sam. 'It's not fair.'

'I'm not mean,' said Camille. 'It's for his own good.'

'You're talking about me as though I wasn't here,' said Tim, 'so I may as well go.' He was not unduly offended, but he was torn between the urge to remind Camille that he often behaved badly in a normal way and the knowledge that this would be childish.

'Don't be such a schmuck,' said Camille. 'Let's go to the wine bar.' She was feeling particularly inhuman today. The prospect of growing up to be a woman like all the other women seemed even more than usually unwelcome, and she could see no way round it. Trying to think of some sort — any sort — of female it would not be too intolerable to resemble, she had constructed a smoking, drinking, lightly promiscuous, careless and irresponsible wit, only to realize that the reason this female seemed somehow familiar was because she had reinvented her grandmother. She wouldn't have minded being like Connie, except that Connie appeared to be enthralled by her Memet, which diminished her attraction and made her seem not to be in full possession of her faculties a lot of the time. The only consolation she could see, slight as it was, was that, at least, she wouldn't turn into a man and have to be like one of them. She began to think that it might be better to be put down like the young greyhounds before your raciness was quite spent, rather than have to grow up and be a drain on the world's resources and a very great bore. Looking round at the many and varied human beings who frequented the Lock she found it insupportable to think that they would take her for one of themselves. Camille's view of her species was jaundiced and probably irrevocable. Reading a woman's magazine in the dentist's waiting-room, which was the only place where she would do such a thing, since she despised these publications, she was surprised to find that a common form of comfort, offered by the savants who dealt with readers' problems, was the reassurance that others suffered similarly, had similar fantasies, and that the correspondent in question was not alone in her affliction. Camille's response to this was that if she could not be individual, even in dolour, then she'd rather be dead. It was not just that she wished to be unique but that the thought of resembling certain people was rather too horrible to be borne. Barbs, for instance: Barbs had always maintained that all were united by a common humanity. Only the ugly and the insecure insisted on this. The beautiful had no need for such nonsense.

'Why d'you look so angry?' asked Sam.

'I'm bored,' said Camille.

'You should've gone to school,' said Tim, rashly.

But Camille only said, 'Don't be silly,' and gazed around despondently. 'If we'd been brought up in a tower block,' she said, 'we'd have something to look forward to, but we already live where everyone wants to live . . .'

'Not everyone,' interrupted Sam.

'Most people,' said Camille. 'Just look at them. They come from all over as though it was Buckingham Palace or Venice Beach or something, not a grotty old lock.'

'They're probably bored too,' said Sam.

'I don't feel a bit sorry for them,' said Camille. 'They make me sick, on the whole.' She glanced at Tim sideways, mutely challenging him to defend the human race against her criticisms. Two policemen in shirt sleeves with muttering machines hung about them strolled unsmilingly past. Camille, with the instincts of a budding bandit, eyed them with reciprocal suspicion.

'There used to be truant officers,' observed Tim. 'They used to go round like dog catchers, collaring kids who weren't in school.' Camille bridled indignantly: this sounded to her like a gross infringement of civil liberties.

'They don't bother now,' said Tim. He sounded regretful, being naturally inclined towards order and discipline as he grew older. He was enjoying a legitimate half-day holiday.

'Public school's had a bad effect on you,' said Sam, reflectively.

'You been brainwashed,' chimed in Camille.

'Shall we run after those two and tell them we know about a missing person?' suggested Sam, invigorated by the thought of a little diversion.

'Don't you dare,' said Tim. 'If they go to Barbs's place, they'll find our fingerprints all over everything and we'll be in deep dog's dos.'

'You should've thought of that before you broke in,' said Sam. Tim didn't deign to reply to this outrageously unfair remark. Even Camille was stirred by its injustice.

'Sam!' she cried.

'Are we going to the wine bar or not?' inquired Sam, unmoved.

'Might as well,' said Camille. 'Hang on – that looks like Con. Here, quick, stand in front of me.'

'I thought you said she wouldn't grass,' said Sam.

'She wouldn't,' said Camille in an unnecessary stage whisper, since Constance was several hundred yards away down the crowded towpath. 'But it's embarrassing for her. She'll begin to worry and think she ought to tell my mum if she starts seeing me all the time.'

'She hasn't seen you,' said Sam. 'They're turning round and going back.'

'Who?' asked Camille.

'Her and Memet,' said Sam. 'He's got his silly hat on.'

'I cannot *imagine* what she sees in that man,' said Camille, in her grandmother's voice.

'He's quite sexy,' said Sam, from the vantage point of a year's seniority and the irresistible urge to contradict her friend.

'Urrgh,' said Camille, over-reacting to this. 'He's *horrible.*'

'I thought you liked him,' said Sam, irritatingly.

'I don't mind him,' said Camille, 'only he's ugly and horrible.'

'He's very attractive to women,' said Sam.

'I think he murdered Barbs,' said Camille. 'I think he murdered her and gave her to his uncle to make into doner kebabs, only he went and forgot his hat and left it in her house. That's what I think.'

'You don't think,' said Sam. 'Not really. You just leap to silly conclusions.'

'You'd better shut up,' said Tim, as Camille opened her mouth, 'or the force will hear you and we'll all be taken in for questioning. If we're going to the wine bar, we might as well go. You can ponce a drink off the barman.'

'I hate the barman,' said Camille.

'You hate everyone,' said Sam, and since, at present, this was the case, Camille didn't argue.

Constance had lost her cool. Close in her sitting-room among the books and the beads, with the windows tight shut against the neighbours, she shook as she questioned her beloved. 'You're sure that was the place?' she said. 'What were the kids doing there? Why were they talking to the police? Eh?'

Memet, by contrast, was perfectly calm. 'Now we've looked at the place again,' he said, 'I see I was imagining it. I'd had a drink or two . . .'

'You mean you were pissed out of your mind,' said Constance, enlightened. Momentarily she felt a weight lift from her. 'That's why you weren't sure what had happened. Not because you weren't looking.'

'Looking back,' said Memet, 'I see that I would have heard if she'd fallen in. There were crowds of people round . . .'

'You said nobody saw you,' said Constance. 'The truth is you don't remember a thing really, do you?'

'I remember getting mad with her,' said Memet.

'That was the drink too,' said Constance. 'You just got paralytic, and when you sobered up you started imagining things.'

'I don't imagine things,' said Memet.

175

'Then you were showing off,' said Constance. 'You were trying to frighten me.'

'Why would I do that?' asked Memet.

'God knows,' said Constance, but she knew too. Fear was an excellent weapon for those who wished to dominate a situation, for frightened people do as they're told and must needs love the frightener. 'You bloody man,' she added.

'If you're going to be like that, I'm off,' said Memet, and Constance breathed deeply.

'Perhaps that would be best,' she said, and cried for a long time until she remembered how often he had gone and had come back.

'. . . so I told him to bugger off,' concluded Constance when she had regaled Scarlet with her story of the evening's events. It was safe to do so now she was convinced that the blood of Barbs did not stain the hands of Memet. 'If people wouldn't tell lies,' she said, 'life would be simpler.'

'It'd be simpler still,' said Scarlet, 'if people weren't so idiotic,' and she began to tell Constance of Brian's version of her relationship with Barbs and the resultant scene. 'He thinks I'm jealous of her,' she said.

'Then he must've fancied her,' said Constance.

'Do you think?' asked Scarlet.

'There's no other reason he'd think you were jealous of her,' explained Constance. 'Even if she looked like the Venus de Milo and was Governor of the Bank of England. They only think you're jealous of the people they fancy.'

'If I thought Brian fancied Barbs,' said Scarlet, 'I wouldn't be jealous of her. I'd think Brian had gone mad, and that'd be sufficient grounds for divorce.'

'They don't see it that way,' said Constance. 'They

never will. It's confusing because so many of them have such ghastly taste in females. Imagine marrying Clarissa, for instance.'

'I'm no oil painting,' said Scarlet. 'I often wonder why two men married me.'

'There's no understanding it,' said Constance, honestly, 'but you don't wipe your lips with your serviette and tell people what the kiddy said over breakfast.'

'I should hope not,' said Scarlet. 'I wonder why everyone thinks they have to go round in twos, like Noah's Ark.'

'That's where the fairy-stories got it wrong,' said Constance. 'The really happy ending is a good secure divorce settlement and a place of your own, out of the wind and the rain's way.'

'You've got a place of your own,' said Scarlet.

'But I got it for myself,' said Constance. 'Not like the fairy-stories, where there's got to be a bit of magic and a bit of dirty work and a couple of flashes of lightning. It's more fun if you wrest it out of adverse circumstances.'

'Such as a husband, you mean?' said Scarlet. 'My mother would have considered herself a total failure if she'd had to work for a living.'

'Ninon de Lenclos,' said Constance. 'I just remembered. She was the old French lady who never gave up.'

'She probably thought it was good for her,' said Scarlet, rather spitefully. 'She probably thought it kept her hormones in trim.'

Constance ignored this. 'You can always come and live with me,' she said, and Scarlet had a moment's ravishing vision of a truer existence, without pretence or striving, in which every Sunday she would have celery and winkles for tea, and Camille would grow up unwarped by the fearful constraints of the middle class. On the other hand, Camille had never shown many signs of being unduly hampered by convention, and Scarlet herself wasn't all that fond of winkles. She was beginning to realize that there was no ideal existence: not for her at any rate. She would go on in the same way until the E additives got her or she died of old age.

'*Now* what are you crying for?' inquired Constance. patiently, and Scarlet said she thought she was suffering from despair.

'Once upon a time,' said Constance, 'I'd've told you to look on the bright side, but I don't think you've got one. You'll have to make one. Use a bit of elbow grease.'

'What you're doing,' said Scarlet, 'is telling me to pull myself together. Aren't you?'

'That's right,' said Constance.

'You can't eat that apple because you haven't washed it,' said Camille. They were sitting on the step outside the Spanish bar watching the market traders.

'You're getting just like your mother,' said Sam, taking a defiant bite.

'You've always been like yours,' said Camille, 'and apples are absolutely covered in poisonous pesticide, and you'll probably drop dead in hideous agony any minute now.'

'I don't care,' said Sam.

'Well, if you don't care, I don't care,' said Camille, and they sat in silence for a while, watching some shabby pigeons picking at the putrefaction in the gutters.

When the bar opened they went in and ordered hot chocolate. 'D'you think we should wash it before we drink it?' said Sam.

'Very funny,' said Camille. 'Anyway, milk's bad for us. They put something in it.'

'They put something in everything,' said Sam. 'Only it was no better in the old days. They put worse things in things then.'

'They hadn't got worse things,' said Camille. 'They keep inventing new ones now.'

'They had arsenic and lead, and they used to grind up the bones of plague victims to put in the bread,' said Sam.

'Why'd they do that?' asked Camille.

'To make the flour go further, silly,' said Sam.

'Sounds dumb to me,' said Camille. 'Sounds like more trouble than it's worth, digging up all those old bones and grinding them. Be cheaper to use more flour, I'd've thought.'

'It was something to do with the repeal of the Corn Laws,' said Sam, authoritatively, and for once Camille couldn't be bothered to argue.

When Tim arrived he brought another boy with him. 'This is Chris,' he declaimed, exhibiting his friend with some pride. Camille surveyed him, sullenly. When they sat down a silence fell.

'So what've you girls been doing?' asked Tim, in order to break it, and Camille cast him a glance of chill contempt.

'We were wondering if we should go to the police,' said Sam, for Barbs's disappearance was still the most interesting thing that had happened for some time.

'Why?' asked Chris.

'Our neighbour's missing,' explained Sam. 'We don't know where she is.'

'She's called Barbs,' contributed Camille, for she had quite liked the way Chris said 'why'.

'No one's got any idea where she's gone,' said Tim.

'I know,' said Chris. They gazed at him, speechlessly.

'My mother went too,' he said. 'They've gone to sort out some refugees. There was a picture of them in the paper a couple of weeks ago, just before they went.'

'Why didn't you tell me?' demanded Tim.

'You didn't ask,' said Chris. 'I could've told you if you'd asked.'

'That's just like you,' said Sam, crossly, to Tim. She was annoyed that their mystery was a mystery no longer and, more obscurely, offended at the realization that Tim had never been as beguiled by it as she had been herself. If he had been, he would have mentioned it to his precious friend. Either he was superior to what he regarded as female gossip or he didn't care, and whichever it was she wasn't pleased with him. 'But she didn't take her make-up,' she said.

'Or her money,' chimed in Camille.

'They don't,' said Chris.

'Well, they wouldn't,' said Tim. 'They wouldn't go round in make-up, flashing their money about. Not where they've gone.'

'You don't know where they've gone,' snapped Sam.

'They've gone . . .,' began Chris.

'I don't care where they've gone,' said Sam. 'I want another hot chocolate. I'm bored with Barbs.'

'Everyone's bored with Barbs,' said Camille. 'Just think of those poor refugees.'

'They'll be pleased to see her,' said Tim, 'if she's taken them things to eat and some blankets.' Camille recognized the reproach implicit in this remark and watched him steadily over the rim of her cup. 'I wasn't,' he said.

'You were,' said Camille.

'She thinks he was being Christian,' explained Sam to Chris. 'It makes her angry.'

'He was just being reasonable,' said Chris. 'It can be annoying, but it's the way he is.'

'I don't care any more anyway,' said Camille. 'He can be Christian if he likes. I'm getting more tolerant.'

'You're probably getting lazier, you mean,' said Sam. 'Can't even be bothered to get mad any more.'

'I haven't got mad for ages,' said Camille.

'It is a few days,' admitted Tim. 'That's quite a time for you.'

'I'm going to be an angel from now on,' said Camille, stretching. 'You can watch.'

'I'll watch,' said Chris. 'I'll tell you when you're going wrong. I've got to go now. I'll be late.'

'Where's he going?' asked Sam, as Chris departed.

'School,' said Tim. 'He's got a strong sense of responsibility.' Camille watched him go. She was enchanted by his offer to watch her but could not, of course, mention this. 'What did you think?' asked Tim.

'What of?' asked Sam.

'Chris,' said Tim.

'He's OK,' said Sam. 'I suppose.'

'I liked him,' said Camille, partly to be contrary in the face of her friend's apathy and partly because she did.

'He reminds me of Brian a bit,' said Sam.

'Oh, don't be so *stupid*,' said Camille, standing on the threshold. 'Let's go and have a margarita.'

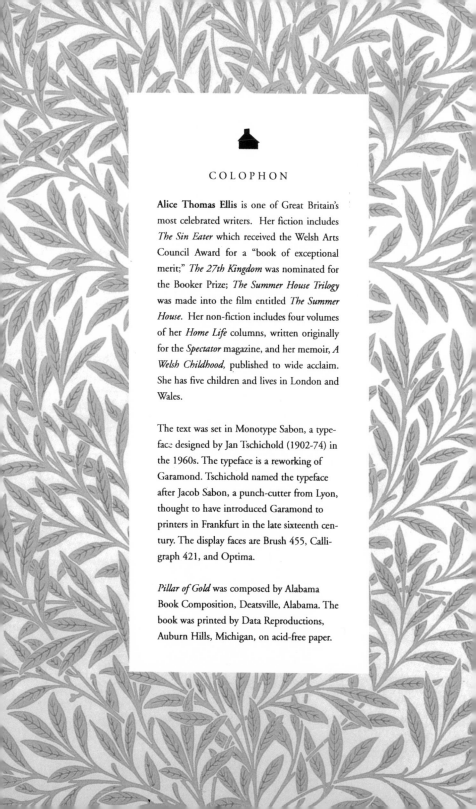

COLOPHON

Alice Thomas Ellis is one of Great Britain's most celebrated writers. Her fiction includes *The Sin Eater* which received the Welsh Arts Council Award for a "book of exceptional merit;" *The 27th Kingdom* was nominated for the Booker Prize; *The Summer House Trilogy* was made into the film entitled *The Summer House.* Her non-fiction includes four volumes of her *Home Life* columns, written originally for the *Spectator* magazine, and her memoir, *A Welsh Childhood,* published to wide acclaim. She has five children and lives in London and Wales.

The text was set in Monotype Sabon, a typeface designed by Jan Tschichold (1902-74) in the 1960s. The typeface is a reworking of Garamond. Tschichold named the typeface after Jacob Sabon, a punch-cutter from Lyon, thought to have introduced Garamond to printers in Frankfurt in the late sixteenth century. The display faces are Brush 455, Calligraph 421, and Optima.

Pillar of Gold was composed by Alabama Book Composition, Deatsville, Alabama. The book was printed by Data Reproductions, Auburn Hills, Michigan, on acid-free paper.